STALLION IN THE STABLE

Mandy stood up and went over to the window. The light was fading but she could still see the ponies in the field.

As Mandy watched them, she became aware of a fleeting movement in the garden below her. She strained her eyes to make out what it was. Perhaps there was a fox or a deer out there.

But it wasn't an animal. It was a person.

'Nick!' Mandy said out loud, recognising him.

Nick seemed to be in a hurry. He was running purposefully across the lawn and carrying a heavy-looking sack in each hand. What could he be up to? Quickly, she grabbed a jacket and headed out of the room. She knocked on James's door. 'James,' she whispered. 'Come quickly.'

Animal Ark series

1 Kittens in the Kitchen
2 Pony in the Porch
3 Puppies in the Pantry
4 Goat in the Garden
5 Hedgehogs in the Hall
6 Badger in the Basement
7 Cub in the Cupboard
8 Piglet in a Playpen
9 Owl in the Office
10 Lamb in the Laundry
11 Bunnies in the Bathroom
12 Donkey on the Doorstep
13 Hamster in a Hamper
14 Goose on the Loose
15 Calf in the Cottage
16 Koalas in a Crisis
17 Wombat in the Wild
18 Roo on the Rock
19 Squirrels in the School
20 Guinea-pig in the Garage
21 Fawn in the Forest
22 Shetland in the Shed
23 Swan in the Swim
24 Lion by the Lake
25 Elephants in the East
26 Monkeys on the Mountain
27 Dog at the Door
28 Foals in the Field
29 Sheep at the Show
30 Racoons on the Roof
31 Dolphin in the Deep
32 Bears in the Barn
33 Otter in the Outhouse
34 Whale in the Waves
35 Hound at the Hospital
36 Rabbits on the Run
37 Horse in the House
38 Panda in the Park
39 Tiger on the Track
40 Gorilla in the Glade
41 Tabby in the Tub
42 Chinchilla up the Chimney
43 Puppy in a Puddle
44 Leopard at the Lodge
45 Giraffe in a Jam
46 Hippo in a Hole
47 Foxes on the Farm
48 Badgers by the Bridge
49 Deer on the Drive
50 Animals in the Ark
51 Mare in the Meadow
52 Cats in the Caravan
53 Polars on the Path
54 Seals on the Sled
55 Husky in a Hut
56 Beagle in the Basket
57 Bunny on the Barge
58 Guinea-pigs in the Greenhouse
59 Dalmatian in the Dales
60 Lambs in the Lane

Plus:
Little Animal Ark
Animal Ark Pets
Animal Ark Hauntings
Animal Ark Holiday Specials

LUCY DANIELS

Stallion — in the — Stable

Illustrations by Ann Baum

a division of Hodder Headline Limited

Special thanks to Andrea Abbott

Thanks also to C. J. Hall, B.Vet.Med., M.R.C.V.S., for reviewing the veterinary information contained in this book.

Created by Working Partners Limited, London W6 0QT
Original series created by Ben M. Baglio

First published in Great Britain in 2002
by Hodder Children's Books

For more information about Animal Ark,
please contact www.animalark.co.uk

10 9 8 7 6 5 4 3

A Catalogue record for this book is available from
the British Library

ISBN 0 340 85153 8

Typeset by Avon Dataset Ltd, Bidford-on-Avon, Warks

Printed and bound in Great Britain by
Clays Ltd, St Ives plc

The paper and board used in this paperback by Hodder Children's Books are natural recyclable products made from wood grown in sustainable forests. The manufacturing processes conform to the environmental regulations of the country of origin.

Hodder Children's Books
a division of Hodder Headline Limited
338 Euston Road
London NW1 3BH

One

As Mandy Hope felt the train slow down, she peered out of the carriage window. There was an old stone building at the side of the railway line and an iron bridge spanning the track. A signboard flashed by.

'Aberford,' Mandy read out loud. She spun round. 'We're here!' she said to her best friend, James Hunter.

'At long last,' said James. He jumped up and began pulling their bags down from the luggage rack. The train gave a loud hoot, signalling its arrival as it drew up alongside a narrow platform.

Mandy picked up her riding hat from the seat and slung it over her arm. A tingle of excitement ran through her. The weeks of waiting were over at last. 'Not long now before we're on horseback,' she said happily.

It was the start of the summer holidays, and Mandy and James had come to the Scottish Highlands for a week of pony trekking at the Kincraig Trekking Centre.

The train lurched to a halt. Mandy grabbed her bag, pushed open the carriage door and climbed down on to the platform. James slung his backpack over his shoulders, then jumped down behind her and slammed the door shut.

'What time did Mrs Russell say she'd pick us up?' he asked. Mrs Russell was the owner of Kincraig.

Mandy shrugged. 'She just said she'd meet our train,' she said.

'Well, she should spot us easily,' said James, glancing up and down the empty platform. 'We're the only ones here.' The train began to move off and James looked anxiously around the deserted station. 'Do you think she's forgotten us?' he wondered.

Mandy shook her head. 'She promised she'd be here.' Beside her, the train gathered speed. 'I expect she's just a bit late,' she added, watching the guard's van go past in a blur.

The train disappeared around a bend, the sound of its wheels fading quickly. Mandy looked across the tracks and saw a green jeep parked near the foot of the bridge. 'You can relax, James,' she grinned. 'We haven't been abandoned! We're just on the wrong side. There's Mrs Russell.'

A short woman with long blonde hair was standing next to the jeep. She waved at them and called out, 'Come over the bridge!'

Mandy and James clattered over the old iron bridge to the other side of the track where Mrs Russell greeted them warmly. 'Welcome to Scotland - especially to the Highlands.' She opened the back of the battered old jeep and they slung their luggage inside. 'Nick would have come down with me but he's out on a ride with two other guests this afternoon,' she explained.

Nick was Mrs Russell's thirteen-year-old son. Mandy had already spoken to him on the telephone. From what Nick had told her, his life revolved around horses and his Rough collie,

Moss. Mandy understood exactly what he meant because she was crazy about animals too. She was even determined to become a vet one day – just like her parents, who ran a veterinary surgery from their home, Animal Ark, in the Yorkshire village of Welford.

'Nick's really looking forward to riding with you,' Mrs Russell said as they all climbed into the jeep. 'He thought the school term would never end!'

'Me too,' James said, sliding across the back seat then sitting back and clipping on his seatbelt.

'Do you have many other guests at the moment?' Mandy asked. She was sitting in the front next to Mrs Russell.

'No, not many,' answered Mrs Russell, steering the jeep down the bumpy lane that led away from the station. 'You see, not a lot of people know about us yet. We only started up in the spring. It'll take a while for people to hear about us.'

'How many ponies do you have?' asked James.

'Seven,' said Mrs Russell, turning off the lane on to a narrow tarred road. 'And they're all gorgeous – although I'm biased of course!'

'I can't wait to see them,' Mandy smiled,

checking her pockets to make sure the polo mints she'd brought from home were still there. 'Is Kincraig a long way from here?'

'About fifteen miles,' said Mrs Russell. 'We'll be there in about half an hour.'

The road took them over a hump-backed bridge across a fast-flowing river, then ran along the shore of a long, thin loch.

'Loch Bonar,' said Mrs Russell. 'Narrow, but very deep.'

'Is there a Loch Bonar monster?' James grinned.

'Certainly! It's a close relative of Nessie – the monster that lives in Loch Ness,' joked Mrs Russell.

Soon, the road veered away from the loch and headed towards a rocky mountain range.

'The North West Highlands,' said Mrs Russell. She pointed to a high peak. 'And that's Ben Beag. Kincraig is in the foothills of Beag.'

'Wow! You really *are* in the Highlands,' said James, gazing out of the window. 'I didn't know we'd be *on* a mountain.'

Mrs Russell chuckled. 'It's certainly mountainous where we are. Ideal terrain for trekking. And you can ride for hours without seeing another soul.'

'Don't you have any neighbours?' Mandy asked.

'Very few,' Mrs Russell told her. 'There's a big stud farm on the other side of Ben Beag and a couple of crofters dotted around. But I think we see more red deer and golden eagles than people!'

Nearing the mountains, the road grew even narrower. Soon the huge grey mass of the Highland range loomed over them as they wound their way through the valley. They approached a tight bend and Mrs Russell slowed down. She glanced in her rear view mirror and frowned. 'He's right on my tail,' she said, shaking her head in irritation. 'What does he think he's playing at?'

Mandy looked round and saw a big pick-up truck behind them, towing a trailer. It was so close that Mandy could see the expression on the driver's face. He glared at them impatiently, as if he was in a hurry.

Mrs Russell pulled over as far as she could. The pick-up swung out then shot past them and cornered the bend at high speed. Behind it, the trailer swayed dangerously from side to side.

Mandy drew in her breath. 'I hope there isn't a horse in there,' she murmured, shuddering.

'So do I,' said Mrs Russell, rounding the corner cautiously.

Just ahead of them, the pick-up hurtled towards the next sharp turn. Mandy found herself pushing her feet against the floor, willing the driver to slow down. And then, as the truck rounded the bend, the trailer veered off the road and bounced wildly along the rough verge for a few metres before dragging the pick-up to a stop.

'The fool!' exclaimed Mrs Russell, slamming on the brakes. 'I *knew* that would happen. We'd better see if he needs any help.'

Anxious that there could be a horse in the trailer, Mandy quickly flung open her door and jumped out of the jeep. James and Mrs Russell leaped out behind her and they ran over to the trailer. A plaintive neigh came from inside.

'There *is* a horse inside!' Mandy cried. 'He could be hurt.'

'Let's open the jockey door and find out,' said James, reaching for the handle of the small door at the side of the horsebox.

'There'll be no need for that,' came a rough voice which stopped James in his tracks. 'The pony will be all right.'

Mandy looked round and saw a stocky man climbing out of the truck. He pushed a grubby-looking tweed cap back from his forehead, then folded his arms and surveyed the box briefly. 'Not too good at road-holding, these horseboxes,' he grumbled.

'You were driving far too fast,' Mrs Russell pointed out.

'No, I wasn't,' retorted the man. 'But I *am* in a hurry. Still, at least there's no damage done. I'll be on my way again.'

From inside the horsebox came another pitiful neigh.

'You ought to check the pony,' Mandy said. 'It sounds distressed.'

But the man ignored Mandy's appeal and turned away. 'There'll be plenty of time to see to him at home,' he said as he strode back to the pick-up.

'How can anyone be so cold-hearted?' Mandy said loudly.

'And what if the pony is seriously injured?' said James, still holding the handle of the jockey door.

Mandy glared at the retreating back of the man. Inside the box, the pony whinnied again. Mandy knew they had no choice. They *had* to make sure it was all right.

Mrs Russell must have been having the same thought because she glanced at the man, who had stopped to check the wheels of the pick-up. 'Quickly, James, open the jockey door,' she said.

James opened the small door and he and Mandy peered inside.

Mandy caught her breath. A young, dapple-grey pony stared dejectedly down at them. Mandy quickly stepped inside. She stretched out her hand to the pony. 'Are you all right?' she said softly.

The pony nuzzled her hand then fixed his big, sad-looking brown eyes on Mandy's face. Mandy took out a few mints and gave them to him. Eagerly the pony took them, munching noisily, while Mandy ran her hand along his side. His coat was thick and shaggy but Mandy could feel his ribs beneath it. She was about to give him another handful of mints when there came the sound of a car door slamming outside.

'Quickly, Mandy,' called James, glancing over his shoulder. 'The man's going.'

Mandy scrambled out and shut the door behind her just as the driver started up the engine and began to pull away. 'I don't think the pony's hurt,' she reported to James and Mrs Russell. 'And he ate the mints I gave him. But he's quite thin.'

The trailer lurched forward then stopped with a jolt as the wheels of the truck started spinning on the soft verge. The man revved the engine loudly. The wheels churned up the ground, sending clods of earth flying.

'He'll never pull away like that,' shouted James above the whine of the engine.

Mrs Russell shook her head in astonishment. 'He's more likely to burn out the motor.'

'And upset the poor pony even more,' said Mandy, looking anxiously at the trailer.

The driver slammed the vehicle into reverse and backed up a few metres. The trailer swung out sharply at a right angle and the man braked, then gunned the motor again.

Above the roar of the engine, there came another neigh.

Mandy's heart was in her mouth. 'He *can't* treat the pony like this,' she said determinedly, dashing forward to beg the man to be more careful.

But at that moment, the wheels of the pick-up found solid ground. The vehicle shot forward, yanking the trailer straight behind it, then roared off in a cloud of black smoke.

They all stared speechlessly after it.

'That poor pony,' Mandy murmured, looking away. It felt almost unbearable to watch helplessly as the trailer bounced wildly along behind the pick-up. All Mandy could do was hope that there would be no more accidents and the pony would reach his destination safely.

Two

'What an unpleasant man,' Mandy said, as they climbed back into the jeep. 'Do you know him?'

'Yes, I'm afraid I do. He's called Angus Mackay,' answered Mrs Russell, turning the key in the ignition. 'He's my neighbour, but we've only met once or twice. He owns the stud farm on the other side of Ben Beag I was telling you about earlier. He breeds Highland Ponies.'

They set off again along the narrow road. There was no sign of the pick-up and trailer, and Mandy began to relax again. Perhaps the accident had jolted Mr Mackay into driving more carefully.

Soon the road turned away from the valley and started winding up the foothills of Ben Beag.

'This is why we need a jeep,' said Mrs Russell, changing to a lower gear. 'It gets pretty steep in places.'

Mandy gazed out at the incredible view. Far below, Loch Bonar sparkled in the sunshine like a silver ribbon. A tiny motorboat skimmed across the surface. Mandy could just make out the form of a water skier leaping over the wake left by the boat.

'That must be some ride,' said James, also spotting the skier.

'But not as good as riding a pony,' Mandy smiled.

The road grew steeper then suddenly took a downward curve. When it straightened out again, they found their way blocked by a small herd of Highland cattle ambling along in front of them.

Mrs Russell braked and drove at a snail's pace behind the shaggy red-haired creatures. From time to time, she had to stop while the cattle nibbled unhurriedly at the gorse and heather growing next to the road.

'We could be stuck behind them for ages,' Mrs Russell sighed after a few minutes. She wound down her window and leaned out. 'Move along, you lot,' she called out.

A large cow turned and stared at them while she quietly chewed the cud.

'She looks as if she's thinking about it,' Mandy laughed.

'As long as she isn't thinking about charging at us with those long horns of hers,' grinned James.

'She probably couldn't be bothered,' smiled Mrs Russell. 'She's too laid back even to get out of our way! Let's see if this works.' She beeped the horn.

The cow blinked at them then, with an exaggerated dip of her enormous head, she turned and lumbered off the road. The rest of the herd gradually followed. Eventually the way was clear again.

'Not much further now,' said Mrs Russell, speeding up a little.

They passed more cattle and several sheep grazing beside the road before finally coming to a big wrought-iron sign. It straddled two stone pillars at the entrance to a dirt road and told them they had arrived at Kincraig.

Minutes later, Mrs Russell pulled up in front of a picturesque old farmhouse, set in the middle of a sprawling green lawn. The grey stone of the house matched the steely colour of the mountain. Pink climbing roses rambled up the walls and around the window frames.

'What a beautiful place!' Mandy exclaimed. She climbed out of the jeep and glanced around for a first sight of the ponies.

'And really quiet,' said James, jumping down on to the gravel which crunched loudly under his feet.

Mandy listened. Apart from the clucking of a few chickens that were pecking in a flowerbed nearby, there wasn't a sound. But, just then, the stillness was broken as the front door opened and two Rough collies came racing out to meet them. One was sable – dark brown – and white and the other was sable, white and black with a blaze on her muzzle.

'Hello, gorgeous dogs,' said Mandy patting the tricolour who sniffed her up and down inquisitively.

'That's Moss,' said Mrs Russell. 'Nick's dog. The other is Fern, her mother. And speaking of Nick – here he is.'

Nick was following the dogs out of the house. Like his mum, he was short with blonde hair. In fact, his wiry build reminded Mandy of a jockey.

'Hi,' he said, smiling broadly. 'The dogs heard the jeep from miles away, ages before I heard it. They've been watching out for you from my bedroom window.'

James grinned. 'Trust a dog to sense things before humans do.'

'Especially Moss,' said Nick. He looked down proudly at her. 'She's going to be a rescue dog.'

Mandy was instantly fascinated. 'You mean she'll find people lost in the mountains?' she asked.

'That's right,' said Nick. 'She's already passed the first four grades in the Search and Rescue Association, and she's going for Grade Five this week. If she passes, she'll have full rescue-dog status.'

'Wow! You *are* an important dog,' said James, giving Moss an appreciative look. 'Will we be able to watch you two in action?' he asked.

'Yes – except that I won't be handling her,' Nick answered. 'You have to be at least thirty-one to do that.'

'So who'll be taking her out?' Mandy asked.

'My Uncle John,' said Nick. 'He's an experienced search and rescue handler but his own dog, Bracken, died a few months ago.' Nick paused then added softly, 'Bracken was Moss's brother. I like to think that she'll be working in memory of him.'

Gently Mandy scratched the top of Moss's head. 'You'll do really well in your test, won't you girl?' she murmured. 'For Bracken's sake.'

'We're all keeping our fingers crossed,' put in Mrs Russell. 'Still, we mustn't get our hopes up too much. Moss can be a bit nervous sometimes – especially when it gets steep. That could be enough to disqualify her.'

Nick nodded glumly but said nothing. Mandy guessed he'd be really disappointed if Moss didn't make the grade.

Mrs Russell clapped her hands together. 'Anyway. Let's not stand around talking all day,' she said cheerfully. 'I'm sure you two must be hungry after your long journey. Grab your bags and we'll go in for some refreshments. We'll introduce you to our other guests – Clare and Rachel. They're on holiday from university. Then you can meet the ponies.'

'Er, we'd really . . .' Mandy began but Nick interrupted her.

'If you're anything like me, you'd rather meet the ponies first,' he grinned.

Mandy laughed. 'Exactly!'

'Just dump your luggage by the door,' said Nick. 'I'll take you straight out to the fields.'

The fields were behind the house. They sloped gently up the mountain and were surrounded by wooden railings. The ponies were at the top of the field closest to the house, grazing the coarse pasture. With the two dogs at their heels, Mandy, James and Nick climbed through the railings and started picking their way over the rough ground. They hadn't gone very far when the ponies spotted them and came trotting down the rocky hillside.

'They're really sure-footed,' Mandy remarked, noticing how they made their way over quite big boulders without stumbling.

'That's why they make such good trekking horses,' said Nick. 'They're also very hardy. They don't even like being stabled.' He pointed to a row of stables near the house. 'But we do bring them in when the weather's really bad.'

The seven ponies clustered around them. Mandy looked from one to the other. They were all so gorgeous, it was going to be difficult to choose just one of them. 'They're really friendly,' she laughed, as a black pony nuzzled her hair then bent its neck to sniff around her pocket. 'And greedy,' she added, taking out a mint.

'That one's called Hunter because he's always hunting round pockets for treats!' Nick told her.

'Hunter!' said James, a look of surprised delight on his face. 'That's my name too.' He shot Mandy a warning glance. 'And don't say it's because I'm greedy as well!'

Mandy grinned at him. 'Would I say that?' she asked innocently.

James wrinkled his nose then fished around in his pocket for a mint. 'I guess it's obvious which pony I'm going to choose for the week,' he said, holding his hand out to the stocky black pony.

With surprising gentleness, Hunter took the mint in his huge teeth. He crunched it up then began sniffing James's pocket for more.

'That's enough for now,' James smiled. 'Otherwise there won't be any left for the rest of the week.'

'Or for the other ponies,' Mandy put in. She turned to Nick. 'What are the others called?'

Nick patted a cream dun mare. 'This is Breeze and that brown one there is Skye,' he said. A powerfully built dapple-grey pony came up to him and nuzzled his arm. 'This one's Grampian . . .'

'Because he's tough like the mountains?' suggested James.

'You've got it,' grinned Nick. He pointed to a chestnut mare. 'That's Spey – after the famous river, because she loves splashing through water. And the palomino is Mary, and last of all,' he reached out and rubbed the shoulders of a young, grey dun pony, 'Zebra!'

'Zebra?' echoed Mandy in astonishment. 'Why?'

'Look at the stripes behind his knees and on his hocks,' said Nick.

'Just like zebra markings,' pronounced James.

'Brilliant name,' laughed Mandy.

James managed to sneak a mint to Grampian without Hunter spotting it. 'This one reminds me a bit of the pony in the horsebox,' he said to Mandy.

'Except Grampian's in much better condition,' she pointed out.

Nick looked puzzled. 'Which pony are you talking about?' he asked.

Mandy told him about the incident with Angus Mackay. Nick listened quietly then bit his lip and said, 'That poor horse. He's not having much luck.'

'Do you know him?' asked James, sounding surprised.

Nick nodded. 'It sounds like Gandalf's Secret. I guess Mr Mackay must have taken him to the horse sale in Aberford today.'

'He must have been on his way back,' Mandy said.

Nick folded his arms across his chest and looked away. At his side, Moss whined softly and nudged his thigh with her long nose.

Nick looked down at her and rubbed her head. 'It's OK, girl,' he said. 'I'm just a bit worried about Gandalf. Things aren't going all that well for him at the moment.'

'What do you mean?' Mandy asked.

'Well, Gandalf wasn't placed in his class at the Aberford show last week,' explained Nick. 'Mr Mackay was quite put out. He loaded Gandalf into his trailer then roared off like a maniac.'

'Sounds familiar,' mused James. He tried to fend off Hunter who was sniffing around his pockets again. 'And now it looks like Mr Mackay's trying to sell Gandalf, but no one wants to buy him.'

'Could be,' said Nick, absent-mindedly patting Moss's back.

Mandy remembered the stallion's sad expression. 'I guess no one wanted to buy such a miserable-looking pony,' she suggested.

'Or he didn't reach his reserve price,' said Nick. 'Mr Mackay is more interested in making money.'

'He sounds worse by the minute,' said James, giving in to Hunter and letting him have another mint. 'I wonder what will happen to Gandalf now?'

Nick shrugged. 'Let's just hope Mr Mackay will put some condition on him before the next sale.' Then, changing the subject abruptly, he reached over and patted Grampian and said, 'I usually ride this little fella, but if you want to choose him, Mandy, that's fine by me.'

Mandy looked at each of the horses again. Finally she made up her mind. 'I'll take Zebra,' she said.

'So that you can tell everyone at home that you

rode a Zebra in the Scottish Highlands?' James laughed.

'Wouldn't that be fantastic publicity for Kincraig?' smiled Nick, sounding more cheerful now. 'Loads of people would come to ride then.'

'And they'd be glad they did when they see that he's such a brilliant pony,' said Mandy, patting Zebra's neck.

'When do we go on our first ride, Nick?' asked James.

'First thing in the morning,' Nick told him. He looked at his watch. 'I'd take you out for a short trek now, but it's nearly suppertime and I still want to work Moss today.' He held on to Moss's collar. 'Would you take Fern back to the house so that Moss and I can practise going down into that valley?' he asked, pointing to the far side of the paddock. Beyond the railings, the land fell steeply away to a narrow river valley.

'Sure,' said Mandy. She slapped her thigh encouragingly. 'Come on, Fern. Come and show us your home.'

Mandy and James headed back to the house with Fern running ahead of them. Inside, the house was more modern than Mandy had expected. The wooden furniture was light and simple, and bright curtains softened the edges of the cottage pane windows.

Mrs Russell was in the living-room reading the *Aberford Herald*. 'Ah, there you are,' she smiled, lowering the paper as they came in. 'I was about to send out a search party for you.'

'You wouldn't have been able to,' joked James. 'Nick and Moss have gone down to the valley.'

Mrs Russell shook her head. 'Nick's getting really worked up about the assessment. He spends hours taking Moss over rough terrain. But I'm not sure how much it's helping. Like people, some dogs just don't like tricky ground. Still, we'll soon find out.' She folded the paper and put it on the coffee table in front of her. 'Now, let me show you your rooms.'

Mandy and James fetched their bags, then followed Mrs Russell upstairs. The walls of the passage leading to the bedrooms were decorated with photographs taken during previous treks.

'It looks brilliant!' James exclaimed, examining a shot of ponies and riders going through a deep ravine.

'It is,' said Mrs Russell enthusiastically. 'You're

going to have a wonderful time.' Then, leaving them to unpack, she went downstairs to organise the evening meal.

Mandy crossed over to the window in her bedroom. She had a perfect view of the paddock and all the ponies. For a while, she watched Hunter cantering about with Breeze and Zebra. She peered across to where they'd last seen Nick and Moss but there was no sign of them.

She turned to begin unpacking and was surprised to see an enormous tabby cat stretched out in the middle of her bed. 'Hello!' she said. 'Who are you?'

The cat stared at her with big green eyes. He yawned lazily then blinked and looked away. Mandy went over and stroked him. The cat stood up and stretched then, with a flick of his fluffy tail, jumped off the bed and sauntered towards the door.

'Sorry!' Mandy called. 'Did I offend you or something?'

Just then, a girl of about seventeen popped her head round the door. 'I wouldn't worry about MacDonald,' she smiled. 'He treats everyone with disdain. But we all adore him! I'm Morag, by the way.'

'Hello, I'm Mandy. Are you Nick's sister?' Mandy asked, although she couldn't remember Mrs Russell saying anything about a daughter.

'No,' answered Morag. 'I work here. I do everything from cooking to grooming.'

'And riding?' Mandy suggested.

'You bet!' said Morag, her eyes sparkling. 'That's why I work here. I'm crazy about horses. I go out on treks too. I'll be joining you in the morning.'

'That'll be great!' said Mandy. 'Will Clare and Rachel be coming too?'

'Not tomorrow,' Morag told her with a broad grin. 'They're rather saddle sore after two days on horseback so they've decided to go hiking instead!'

Mandy noticed the cat peering in at the door behind Morag. 'Don't look now,' she whispered, 'but I think MacDonald's about to grace us with his presence again!'

'Oh, we are privileged.' Morag smiled as the cat strolled into the room. Without looking at them, he jumped on to the window sill then sat with his back to them and gazed out at the horses.

'Arrogant moggy!' laughed Morag as she turned

to go. 'Supper will be ready in about half an hour,' she said.

When Mandy and James went down to the dining room, they found Mrs Russell already at the table, tossing a big green salad in a glass bowl. Clare and Rachel were there too and Mrs Russell introduced them to the newcomers.

'You must be starving,' Mrs Russell said when they were all seated at the table.

'James is *always* starving,' Mandy chuckled. 'Just like his namesake, Hunter!'

James pulled a face at her. 'I knew you'd find the chance to say something like that,' he said with a grin. His eyes lit up as Morag came in carrying a steaming dish of pasta with a cheese and mushroom sauce.

'Nick's still not back,' said Mrs Russell, piling a big heap of spaghetti on to James's plate. 'But we won't wait for him. He's often out till nightfall, practising with Moss.'

Mandy helped herself to salad then passed the bowl to Clare. Just then, she felt something brush against her leg. She looked down into a pair of bright green eyes. 'Hello, MacDonald,' she grinned.

The tabby blinked then jumped on to Nick's empty chair beside Mandy and began to purr loudly.

'Well, how about that!' exclaimed Mrs Russell. 'It seems you've won him over, Mandy!'

Three

The ground was still soaked in dew when Mandy and James were getting ready to go out to the fields the next morning.

Nick wasn't up yet, so Mrs Russell suggested that Mandy, James and Morag take their ponies to the stable yard to tack them up in the meantime. 'There are some headcollars and lead ropes hanging in the back porch,' she told them before going upstairs to make sure Nick was awake.

The three of them pulled on their riding boots at the back door then went out to the ponies. They were just climbing through the railings when Nick joined them.

'Hi,' he said cheerfully. 'Sorry I'm late.' He took a bite out of an apple. 'Breakfast on the run this morning,' he grinned. He ducked under the railings and whistled shrilly.

The ponies were grazing at the far side of the paddock. They looked up immediately then trotted over to the fence.

'As obedient as dogs,' chuckled James.

'*All* dogs?' Mandy reacted with a look of mock surprise.

'OK – *some* dogs,' replied James. 'And definitely not Blackie!'

'Who's Blackie?' asked Morag.

'My Labrador,' James told her. 'He's really – er . . .' he glanced at Mandy, '. . . lively. Isn't he, Mandy?'

Mandy raised her eyebrows. Blackie was more than lively. He was probably the most disobedient dog in Welford! 'I think you could say he's not very well trained yet,' she grinned. 'Oh, and talking about training,' she added, turning to Nick, 'how did Moss do yesterday?'

'Moss?' Nick frowned. 'Oh! You mean when I took her into the valley to practise?'

Mandy nodded. 'Was she good on the steep slopes?' she asked.

'I guess so,' said Nick, fiddling with a knot in his leading rein. He put his hand over his mouth and tried to stifle a yawn but couldn't.

'You must have come in really late,' said James. 'I didn't even hear you.'

'Mmm – we had a really long session,' Nick answered. 'But it was worth it. Here, Grampian,' he called, going over to the pony. He slipped the headcollar over Grampian's head then attached the lead rope.

Mandy and James did the same with Zebra and Hunter. Zebra shook his head and stamped his feet as Mandy tried to clip the rein to the headcollar. 'Steady, boy,' she said soothingly. She held the lead rope firmly and rubbed Zebra's neck with her other hand.

'He's just excited,' said Nick, coming to help her. 'He really loves trekking.'

Mandy was pleased to hear this. 'That means I won't have any trouble getting him going,' she smiled.

'Hardly!' said Nick. 'Just wait till he's saddled up. You won't be able to hold him back!'

Morag put a headcollar on Breeze and then, when they were all ready, Nick swung open the gate and they led the four ponies to the stable yard. They fetched bridles and saddles from the tack room and began to tack up the ponies.

Zebra stood surprisingly patiently while Mandy slipped the reins over his head and gently put the bit in his mouth. 'Good boy,' she said to him as she buckled the noseband then reached for a numnah. She lay the soft cloth across Zebra's back. 'Now for the saddle,' she said.

She lifted the saddle high up on to Zebra's neck then pushed it down into place on top of the numnah. 'Comfortable?' she murmured softly as she lifted the saddle flaps to do up the girth.

Zebra snorted and stamped his feet eagerly. Mandy put her foot in the stirrup then swung up on to the pony's broad back. 'I'm ready!' she announced, gathering up the reins.

'No, you're not,' grinned Morag. She gave Mandy a leather saddlebag. 'Lunch,' she said. 'You definitely don't want to go without that.'

'Thanks,' Mandy said, taking the saddlebag and buckling it on to one of the o-rings on the front of the saddle. 'I'd forgotten all about food.'

'Not like someone else,' said James, mounting Hunter then leaning forward and patting the handsome pony's neck. 'I had to give him just about all my mints while I was tacking him up!'

At last, they were ready.

Nick clicked his tongue. 'Let's go, Grampian,' he said.

Mandy squeezed her legs against Zebra's sides. As Nick had said, Zebra needed little encouragement. The pony set off at once, eager to get past Grampian who was at the head of the little group.

'Whoa!' Mandy laughed, holding him back. 'We're not leading the trek. Nick and Grampian are.'

They clattered across the cobblestoned stable yard then crunched up the gravel drive towards the house.

'We need to tell Mum which way we're going,' explained Nick, glancing over his shoulder at the others. 'Just in case someone has to go out looking for us.'

Morag drew up alongside Mandy. 'But that's extremely unlikely,' she added. 'In the mountains you're safer on a Highland pony than you are on foot.'

Mrs Russell was waiting for them at the back door with Moss and Fern at her side. The dogs whined softly and wagged their tails expectantly. Mrs Russell held their collars tightly. 'No, girls,' she said. 'You're staying at home with me. Nick and the others will have enough to think about without having to keep an eye on you two.' She looked at Nick. 'Which route are you taking?'

'The contour path going west round the mountain,' Nick told her, adjusting his riding hat.

'That means I can expect you back by six o'clock,' confirmed Mrs Russell.

'About then,' Nick agreed. 'Even earlier, maybe, because I want to practise with Moss again.'

'Well, have a wonderful day everyone,' said Mrs Russell, as they moved off. 'And take care.'

They retraced their steps down the driveway then turned on to a well-worn path that meandered gradually up the side of the mountain.

Mandy admired the strength of the ponies as they carried their riders over the rocky terrain. Even on the steep slopes, the sturdy little horses kept up a steady pace. And when the ground was flat and even, they were always ready to break into a brisk trot.

After half an hour, Mandy looked back over her shoulder. Kincraig was now just a tiny spot nestling in the valley far below them. 'We've gone miles already,' she remarked to James who was riding behind her.

The path grew steeper then levelled out again. Ahead, a dark green expanse awaited them.

'Pine forest coming up,' called Nick from the front. 'Great place to let the horses have their heads.' He kicked Grampian on and soon they were all cantering through the shady forest.

'This is brilliant!' Mandy cried as Zebra galloped over the soft pine needles. Behind her, she heard a yell of delight from James as the horses gathered speed, their hooves thundering across the forest floor.

They cantered on into a gentle breeze that fanned Mandy's face. The wind stirred the pine needles, making the forest shimmer and whisper all around them.

Mandy was exhilarated. 'This is one of the best rides I've ever had,' she said when they came out of the forest and paused to let the ponies draw breath. 'I hope we get the chance to do that again.'

'We will,' Nick assured her. 'There are lots of forests on Ben Beag.'

'Is that a farm down there?' asked James, pointing down the slope.

A few hundred metres below, a number of buildings and several large paddocks sprawled across a valley. Dozens of horses dotted the paddocks.

'Yes,' said Nick. 'That's Heathwylde – Angus Mackay's stud farm.'

'Let's take a closer look,' suggested Mandy. 'We might even be able to spot Gandalf.'

'Not a good idea,' said Morag seriously. 'The way down is just a bit too steep for my liking.'

Nick agreed. 'The going is much better this way,' he said, turning Grampian and heading away from the farm.

They went on a little further, then stopped for lunch next to a bubbling stream. With their saddles and bridles taken off, the ponies drank thirstily from the river then cropped the coarse grass growing on the hillside. Their riders sprawled out on the ground and tucked into their lunch.

'Brilliant picnic, Morag,' James said appreciatively as he unwrapped a bar of chocolate.

The afternoon ride turned out to be just as thrilling as the morning one. They clambered up and down steep slopes and came close to red deer several times. But even the sure-footed ponies couldn't keep up with the big deer, which fled nimbly into the distance as soon as they spotted the trekkers.

It was after five o'clock when the group arrived back at Kincraig that afternoon. Pleasantly tired from their long, rewarding day, they rubbed the ponies down, then let them loose in the fields.

'Thanks, boy,' said Mandy, giving Zebra a last mint. 'You were brilliant. See you tomorrow.'

She followed the others down to the house. While they were taking their boots off at the back door, they heard voices coming from inside.

'I wonder who's here?' Nick frowned. 'That doesn't sound like Clare and Rachel.'

Morag looked puzzled too. 'Your mum didn't say anything about any new guests,' she said.

The visitor turned out to be a policeman. He was talking to Mrs Russell in the hallway.

'Oh good, just in time,' said Mrs Russell when she saw them coming in. 'Sergeant Campbell's here on behalf of Mr Mackay. Apparently Gandalf's Secret has gone missing from Heathwylde.'

'Gandalf!' Mandy echoed. She could hardly believe that the pony was in trouble yet again.

'Aye. Angus rang the station and reported that the pony's been stolen,' said the sergeant.

'But why would someone want to steal Gandalf and leave all the other horses behind?' asked James with a puzzled look on his face.

Nick was crouching down, patting Moss who'd

come running in from the living room to greet him. 'Even if someone *did* want to steal Gandalf, it's almost *impossible* to get into Heathwylde – let alone steal a horse there,' he pointed out quietly. 'Mr Mackay doesn't welcome trespassers.'

'I wouldn't know about that,' said Sergeant Campbell. 'I'm not saying the horse *has* been abducted. But I have to explore all possibilities. He might just have escaped from Heathwylde so I'm asking people to be on the lookout for him.'

'Well, he's not here,' said Nick quickly. 'We've only got seven ponies and they're all in the field.' He stood up and reached for a light fabric harness that was hanging behind the door. 'Come on, Moss,' he said, putting it on her, 'Let's go out for some practice.'

'You'll keep an eye out for the horse, won't you?' asked Sergeant Campbell as Nick turned and hurried out of the hall.

'Sure,' Nick called.

The sergeant turned to Mandy and James. 'Mrs Russell tells me you two will be out trekking all week,' he said.

They nodded.

'In that case, let me know if you spot a dapple-grey stallion anywhere,' he said. 'Angus tells me it's a valuable horse, and we need to get it back.'

That night, Mandy lay awake in bed, worrying about Gandalf. What if he *had* escaped from Heathwylde? If he was wandering about Ben Beag all on his own, he'd be vulnerable, especially since he wasn't in very good condition.

Somewhere in the house, a clock chimed eleven. Mandy smoothed MacDonald who was curled up next to her, then turned over and willed herself to fall asleep. She wanted to be fresh for the trek in the morning, especially now that they needed to be on the alert for the missing stallion.

She was just drifting off to sleep, when she heard footsteps on the landing then the sound of someone tiptoeing past her room. A door creaked open at the end of the passage.

'Is that you, Nick?' came Mrs Russell's voice.

'Yes,' whispered Nick. 'Sorry. Did I wake you, Mum?'

'Yes,' she murmured. 'Do you *really* have to work Moss so late?'

'Uh-huh,' Nick replied. 'Only a day to go, remember.'

Mandy heard another door open and close and then there was silence. Nick's really keyed up about the assessment, she thought to herself. But surely it was dangerous to be out alone on the mountain at night? Mandy just hoped all the extra practice was worth it.

Four

Nick looked rather preoccupied when they set off on the trek in the morning. He rode a few lengths ahead of Mandy and James, saying very little, only glancing over his shoulder from time to time to make sure they were keeping up.

James drew up alongside Mandy. 'Do you think Nick's OK?' he asked quietly.

Mandy shrugged. 'Maybe he's just tired,' she murmured. 'And nervous about Moss's assessment tomorrow.'

'I guess so,' agreed James, pulling back behind Mandy as they began picking their way through an area cluttered with large boulders. 'I know I'd be nervous if Blackie was doing something like that,' he said.

Mandy burst out laughing. 'Sorry, James,' she said. 'I just can't imagine Blackie actually *rescuing* people. He'd probably jump all over them, trying to make them throw him a stick!'

James saw the funny side too. 'And if they didn't, he'd just stand and bark at them,' he laughed.

Nick had slowed down to allow them to catch up so he had overheard them joking. It seemed to lift his spirits. 'At least that way, Blackie might alert the search team – even if he didn't mean to,' he chuckled.

He turned Grampian off the narrow path they'd been following and looked back at Mandy and James. 'The easy part's over,' he warned them. 'We're going cross-country from now on.'

Mandy's first thought was that this might give them a good chance of spotting Gandalf. She urged Zebra on until they were alongside Nick. 'Do you think Gandalf would let us lead him home if we come across him?' she asked.

Nick stared straight ahead. 'There's no way we'll

see him,' he said firmly. 'And even if we do, I'd rather leave him on the mountain than take him back to Mr Mackay.'

Mandy wasn't sure she agreed with him. Still, she said nothing to Nick. He seemed rather upset about the pony. She didn't want to make matters worse by arguing with him.

They continued over the rough terrain, splashing through streams and squelching through marshy areas.

Mandy looked around. To their right, the land sloped up steeply to a rocky outcrop. 'I bet the view's good from up there,' she said to James.

'Yes, if you're a mountain goat,' grinned James. He lifted his binoculars and scanned the mountainside. 'I wonder what that is?' he said, reining Hunter in and focusing on something down in the valley to their left.

'What?' asked Mandy, looking round.

'There's a sort of hut or something down there,' said James. 'Let's check it out.'

'Oh, that's just an old stable,' said Nick quickly. 'It's not worth going all that way to see it. And anyway, it's really out of our way.' He pointed to the outcrop above them. 'We're going up there.

There's a platform on top and it's the best picnic spot on the mountain.'

Mandy stared doubtfully at it. 'We'll *never* be able to ride up there,' she said.

'No. But we can leave the ponies to graze while we climb up there,' said Nick.

'I thought we were *trekking* through the mountains, not *climbing* them,' James protested good-naturedly.

They rode the ponies up the steep slope as far as they could then dismounted at the bottom of the craggy cliff.

'This is the way up,' said Nick, easing himself through a narrow gap in the rocks then pulling himself on to a narrow ledge.

Gingerly, Mandy and James clambered up the cliff behind him. At the top, they stood and looked around them in wonder. They could see for miles.

'It feels like we're on top of the world,' said Mandy. 'Lend me your binoculars, James.'

James handed them over to her and she trained them on the valley below. 'There are lots of sheep down there,' she said, scanning the landscape slowly. The old stable they'd seen earlier came into view, although it was a long way off.

'Who owns the stable?' she asked Nick.

'No one as far as I know,' replied Nick. Then he groaned. 'Oh no! I just realised. We forgot to bring our lunch up with us.'

They looked down. At the bottom of the cliff, the three ponies nibbled at tufts of grass. And on their backs were the saddlebags – with the lunch!

'I don't believe it!' said Nick. 'We came up here for nothing!'

'No we didn't,' said James. 'We don't have views like this in Welford. And anyway,' he paused, while he rummaged about in his pockets, 'we can always have a mint for lunch!'

Back at Kincraig at the end of the day, Mrs Russell came out to the stable yard to help them unsaddle the ponies. 'No sign of Gandalf, I suppose?' she asked, brushing off Hunter's saddle marks while James took the saddle and bridle into the tack room.

'No,' said Mandy. 'The only animals we saw today were sheep, sheep and more sheep!'

Nick glanced at his watch. 'Hey! It's really late,' he exclaimed. 'Moss and I'd better get going soon.'

He clipped on the leading rein and started to lead Grampian out of the yard.

Mrs Russell stopped brushing Hunter and put her hands on her hips. 'Now hold on just one minute, Nick,' she said sternly. 'You're not going anywhere this evening.'

Nick turned and looked at her in disbelief. 'But it's the last night before the assessment,' he protested.

'Exactly!' retorted Mrs Russell. 'And that's why you should let Moss have a break.' She started brushing Hunter again. 'Even Uncle John thinks it's not necessary to take her out tonight.'

'Did he come over today?' asked Nick.

'He did indeed,' said Mrs Russell. She gave James the body brush so that he could finish grooming Hunter. 'He spent some time with Moss in the field and reckons she's in good shape.'

'Does that mean he thinks she'll pass?' asked Nick eagerly.

Mrs Russell shrugged. 'He didn't quite say that,' she said. 'But he did say she's as ready as she'll ever be.'

A look of delight spread across Nick's face. 'That's brilliant,' he said happily. Then, almost in the same breath, he asked, 'So what's for supper tonight, Mum?'

Mrs Russell winked at Mandy and tried to keep a serious expression. 'In honour of your presence at the table, and because it's Morag's day off, we're having pine needles and gravel sauce!' she told him.

'Oh good! My favourite,' laughed Nick as he led Grampian out of the yard to the paddock. 'I can't wait.'

'You won't have to,' Mrs Russell called out to him. 'It's ready.'

Mandy and James took Zebra and Hunter out to the paddock too, then went back to the house to wash and change before supper.

Later, when everyone was sitting round the table in the dining room, Mrs Russell asked them what they planned to do that evening.

'Not much,' answered Nick, scooping up the last dollop of ice cream in his bowl. He stifled a yawn. 'I think I'll just go to bed early.'

Clare and Rachel were planning to continue a game of chess that they'd started the previous evening. 'I want to keep going while I've got a chance of winning,' smiled Clare.

'And you two?' asked Mrs Russell, turning to Mandy and James.

'Well, I was going to keep a diary of our holiday,' said Mandy, 'and I haven't even started yet. So I think I'll get going on that.'

'And I'm going to read the new computer magazine I brought with me,' said James. 'Dad and I want to upgrade our PC so I'm checking out the latest hardware.'

Mrs Russell looked impressed. 'Sounds complicated,' she said.

'Not for James.' Mandy grinned. 'He's mad about computers.'

They helped Mrs Russell to wash up then went up to their rooms. Mandy sat on her bed and opened the blank diary. But she couldn't concentrate. Her mind was full of ponies and panoramic views and she could still feel the undulating rhythm of Zebra carrying her over the rugged terrain.

Finally she put down her pen and closed the book. 'I'll try tomorrow,' she said. She stood up and went over to the window. The light was fading but she could still see the ponies in the field. Zebra was standing next to Mary, nibbling her neck affectionately.

As Mandy watched them, she became aware of a fleeting movement in the garden below her. She strained her eyes to make out what it was. Perhaps there was a fox or a deer out there.

But it wasn't an animal. It was a person.

'Nick!' Mandy said out loud, recognising him.

Nick seemed to be in a hurry. He was running purposefully across the lawn towards the far side of the paddock where it dipped down into the valley.

Mandy noticed he was carrying a heavy-looking sack in each hand. What could he be up to? Quickly, she grabbed a jacket and headed out of the room. She knocked on James's door. 'James,' she whispered. 'Come quickly.'

James opened the door and Mandy told him what she'd just seen. 'Let's follow him,' she said.

They tiptoed down the stairs, then walked quietly past the living room where Mrs Russell was watching TV. Mandy kept her fingers crossed, hoping the dogs wouldn't hear them going past.

But the dogs must have been soundly asleep because Mandy and James were soon outside without being detected.

'We'll have to hurry,' Mandy told James as they broke into a run past the paddocks. 'He's got a good start on us.'

They scrambled down the rocky slopes that led down into the valley. Mandy caught her foot between two boulders and nearly fell but managed to save herself by grabbing on to a small bush. 'Phew! That was close,' she breathed, steadying herself once more. She peered down the slope. 'I can't see him, can you, James?'

'Not yet,' said James.

They clambered on and finally reached the bottom.

'Now which way?' asked James, looking up and down the swift stream that tumbled past them.

'Over there!' Mandy whispered, pointing across the river to where Nick was emerging from a dense thicket. She noticed that he had managed to tie the sacks to his belt so that he could use his hands when climbing down the slope.

Nick started heading up the valley. Mandy and James crossed the stream then furtively followed him along the river bank. After what seemed like ages, they came to another rocky slope and Mandy spotted Nick just as he disappeared over the top.

'Where on earth is he going?' grunted James as they battled their way up the jagged boulders.

'I think I have a pretty good idea,' said Mandy pulling herself up on to the topmost rock and seeing a field stretching out ahead of them. She knew exactly where they were, for in the middle of the field was a stable. The same one they'd seen from the top of the mountain earlier that day.

By now, Nick had reached the stable. He glanced round once but didn't see Mandy and James. Then he opened the stable door.

The door creaked open and Nick slipped inside. And at that moment, a dapple-grey Highland pony peered out. It looked oddly familiar . . .

'Gandalf!' Mandy burst out. 'Nick's hiding Gandalf's Secret!'

Five

'Nick! What's going on?' Mandy called, as she and James ran up to the stable.

Nick reappeared in the doorway. He stared at them aghast. 'What are you doing here?' he asked, casting an anxious look at the field behind them.

'It's OK,' James reassured him. 'It's only us. We followed you here.'

'But how did you know . . .?' Nick began.

'I saw you running through the paddock,' Mandy told him. She reached forward and patted the side of the pony's neck. 'I should have guessed you were the one who stole Gandalf. You seemed really upset about him.' She frowned at Nick. 'You'll get into big trouble if anyone finds out. What are you going to do?'

Nick shook his head slowly. 'I don't know,' he said, an anxious look crossing his face. 'But I just *had* to get him away from Mr Mackay.'

'Because of the near-miss in the horsebox?' asked James.

'Well, that's what made me go and check on him,' Nick said. 'You see, I've been really worried about him ever since the show when Mr Mackay was angry about him not being placed.' He rubbed the pony's shoulders. 'I didn't tell you this before,' he said quietly, 'but I actually saw Mr Mackay hit him when he was loading him into the trailer.'

Mandy was lost for words. How could anyone hit a pony simply because it didn't do well at a show? And then she remembered how heartless Mr Mackay had seemed after the trailer had gone off the road.

Nick went on. 'When you told me about the accident, I had to make sure Gandalf was OK.' He took out a handful of pony nuts from one of the sacks. Gandalf reached forward with his velvety muzzle and gathered up the pellets.

'And all the time, we thought you were out practising with Moss,' said James, shaking his head slowly.

'We were practising, in a way,' said Nick. A faint smile lit up his eyes for a moment. 'Don't forget, it's pretty tough trekking across the mountain on foot. *And* we were on a rescue mission.'

'So you planned to take Gandalf's Secret away all along?' Mandy asked.

Nick shook his head while he tipped the rest of the pony nuts into a bucket on the ground. The hungry stallion promptly plunged his head into the pail and noisily munched the pellets.

'I didn't know what I was going to do,' Nick confessed. 'But when I found him, I was really shocked. There was no way I could have left him there, even for another minute.'

'Why not?' Mandy asked, trying to imagine how bad things must have been to make Nick take such drastic action.

'Because he was in a tiny field with no water,' said Nick bitterly. As he spoke, he ran his hands through Gandalf's shaggy coat. 'And it was clear that nobody had groomed him for ages. Not only that, but he was lame and no one had done anything about it. That's when I knew I had to take him away.' He pointed to Gandalf's right leg and Mandy noticed for the first time that it was bandaged.

'Who put the bandage on?' she asked.

'I did. Last night,' said Nick. 'Something had punctured the sole of his foot – probably a nail that was lying around the paddock – and he was in a lot of pain.' He passed his hand across his forehead. 'I was worried I'd make the injury worse by bringing him all the way here, but I didn't know what else to do.'

Mandy realised that Nick had been faced with a difficult dilemma. Even though Highland ponies had hard feet and could cope with the roughest ground, a punctured sole could lead to a serious infection. Left untreated, Gandalf would have been in agony.

'I suppose there wasn't any point in telling Mr Mackay,' James put in. 'If he wasn't even worried when the trailer went off the road, he probably wouldn't have cared too much about an injured foot.'

'And he'd have been furious that I'd been on

his land,' said Nick. 'There are big signs everywhere warning that trespassers will be prosecuted!' He went over to the door and looked out. 'I know I should have told my mum what was going on, but I just couldn't walk away and leave Gandalf there that night.'

Mandy nodded sympathetically. If she'd been the one to find the stallion, she might have acted on the spur of the moment like that too. She bent down and felt Gandalf's leg. It was hot to the touch. 'I think he's still in trouble,' she said, straightening up. 'Did you put anything on his foot, Nick?'

'Not yet,' he said, turning and coming back over to the pony. He picked up the other bag he'd been carrying and opened it. 'But I've got a kaolin poultice and some clean dressings in here.'

'Perfect,' said Mandy. 'That should prevent any infection setting in.' She tried to lift Gandalf's foot but he snorted and backed away. Mandy stood up and smoothed his muzzle, saying softly, 'It's all right, Gandalf, we're just trying to help you.'

'It's not going to be easy,' said Nick. 'He wasn't too happy when I put the bandage on last night.

Still, seeing as he hasn't been fed properly for ages, he's not as strong as he could be.' He took out the poultice, which looked like a lump of white putty. 'Let's soak this first while we try to calm him down.'

While James took the old bucket out to a stream that ran through the field behind the stable, Mandy and Nick spoke soothingly to the pony. Gradually, Mandy ran her hand down Gandalf's leg until she was able to touch his injured foot without making him jump. 'The real test will come when we remove the bandage and try to apply the poultice,' she told Nick, resting her hand on the pony's foot for a moment then straightening up and stroking his wiry mane.

James returned and took the poultice out of its plastic bag, then soaked it in the clean water. Then he trained his torch on Gandalf's foot while Nick gingerly lifted the leg and began to peel off the bandage.

All the while, Mandy continued to talk soothingly to Gandalf. When the foot was at last exposed, she bent down and looked closely at the sole. She could see where the nail had gone in. The area was very puffy. 'Poor Gandalf,' she said.

'It must be really tender. Let's just hope it's not already badly infected.'

'I brought a hoof knife to pare down his hoof and clear out any pus,' said Nick, still supporting the stallion's leg in his hands. 'But I don't think he's going to let us do that. We'll just have to apply the poultice and hope for the best.'

As if to show that Nick was right, Gandalf flinched and tried to pull his hoof away.

'Ssh,' said Mandy, running her hands down his neck. 'We won't hurt you.'

Nick waited for a few moments until the stallion had calmed down again then he asked James to pass him the poultice.

'You'll have to hold his leg while I put it on,' Nick said to James. 'And Mandy, just keep on talking to him like that. He seems to listen to you.'

Very carefully, Nick wrapped the dressing around Gandalf's hoof, then applied a thick wad of cotton wool to keep it in place. The stallion flinched once or twice, but Mandy managed to keep him calm.

'We'll have to use the plastic bag to cover his foot,' Nick said when the poultice was firmly in place.

James handed him the bag and Nick carefully pulled it over Gandalf's foot and tied it in place with some sellotape.

At last, the treatment was over. Nick carefully lowered Gandalf's foot to the ground then stood back. 'Well boy, how does that feel?' he asked.

Gandalf looked at Nick then shook his head and whinnied loudly.

'I think he's thanking you,' Mandy grinned.

'Don't mention it, Gandalf,' laughed Nick.

'At least that's one problem solved,' said James.

He switched off his torch and put it back in his pocket.

The sudden murkiness made Mandy feel very isolated. 'It's so lonely out here,' she murmured. She looked out of the door into the dusky night. Not a single light twinkled in the gloom. And all around, the dark bulk of the mountains rose up in eerie silence. Mandy shivered. It was so different from the daytime when the landscape seemed to invite people to come and explore every nook and cranny.

She turned back to Gandalf and smoothed his tousled mane. 'You know you can't keep him here for long, Nick,' she said quietly. 'You'll have to tell your mum eventually.'

'I know,' sighed Nick, picking up the bucket. 'But not just yet.'

'Why not?' asked James. 'You're going to have to own up sometime. You might as well do it now.'

Nick shook his head firmly. 'No. Things are just too complicated right now.'

'You mean with Moss's assessment coming up?' Mandy asked.

'Uh-huh,' murmured Nick. 'I just need to get through that, then I might be able to work something out.' Wearily, he rubbed his eyes with one hand. 'And Gandalf needs more time too. So that he has a chance to get a bit stronger if . . .' he lowered his voice and added sadly, 'he has to go back to Heathwylde.'

'*When* he goes back to Heathwylde,' Mandy said quietly but firmly. They had to face facts. People couldn't go round stealing horses – even if they weren't in good shape. And seeing as Mr Mackay had reported Gandalf missing, he'd find out sooner or later what had happened. And then what? Mandy asked herself silently. What will he do with a pony that he doesn't really care about?

Nick went out to collect some clean water for Gandalf. He came back and put the bucket in the far corner of the stable. 'I think we'd better go home now,' he said. 'Just in case Mum finds out we're not there.' He looked nervously at Mandy and James. 'Promise you won't say anything to her?'

'Promise,' said James.

'As long as *you* promise to tell her as soon as the assessment's over,' Mandy added.

'It's a deal,' said Nick. He picked up the two bags he'd brought with him then put one arm around Gandalf's neck. 'We'll be back tomorrow night, boy.'

Mandy gave the stallion a last pat. 'And hopefully your foot will feel better by then,' she said, trying to sound cheerful but feeling bad about leaving him on his own for another twenty-four hours.

There was a lot to do the next day. Moss's assessment took place over two days and involved her going out on at least two search runs each day. The first run was scheduled for late that morning, so they couldn't join Clare and Rachel on their trek before they went home later that afternoon.

But to take his mind off the looming test, Nick suggested they go out for a short ride before Uncle John arrived to fetch them all.

'Let's go for another canter in that pine forest,' Mandy suggested, while they were tacking up the ponies.

Nick grinned at her. 'I bet that's just an excuse to have another look at Heathwylde.'

Mandy couldn't deny this. 'After everything you've told us about Mr Mackay, I'm really curious about him and his farm,' she confessed. 'Ready, boy?' she said to Zebra. The pony stamped one foot as if he understood. Mandy swung herself up into the saddle.

'We won't need to trespass,' said James, holding up his binoculars as they started out of the stable yard. 'We'll be able to get a really good look at the place without going near it.'

They went past the house, calling to Mrs Russell to tell her the direction they were heading in. 'We won't be long,' Nick reassured his mum as she waved to them from the front door. 'We won't have enough time to take the long forest route,' he said to Mandy and James. 'But I know a path that goes quite close to Heathwylde. It's flat for a lot of the way so we'll be able to go quite fast.'

They walked in single file along the road, then struck out across the fields until they joined a narrow path. The track took them steadily downhill for ten minutes before levelling out, allowing them to break into a fast trot.

Before long, Nick pulled up. 'We'd better not go any closer,' he said.

Mandy and James drew alongside him. They were on the crest of a small hill and just below them was a broad moor that was divided into several paddocks. In the paddocks were dozens of Highland ponies.

'Heathwylde,' Mandy breathed. She soon realised that Gandalf was not the only one of Mr Mackay's ponies to be poorly treated. In the narrow paddock nearest to them, there were six thin, but heavily pregnant mares. Their hip and rib bones were visible and they were standing next to a trough of very dirty water.

'Oh no!' exclaimed Mandy. 'How can he *do* that?'

'Very easily, it seems,' said Nick, staring grimly at the scene before them. 'Even I didn't know things were *this* bad. The last time I came this way in the daytime, I couldn't stop because Mr Mackay was walking around the paddocks. And the other night, I didn't have time to inspect all the ponies. I just grabbed Gandalf and made a run for it before someone saw me.' He pointed to another small paddock at the bottom of the hill. 'Look there.'

A group of ponies was clustered together in one corner of the field. They stretched their necks over the railings and gazed wistfully towards the open moors that surrounded the stud farm.

James looked at them through his binoculars. 'There's not nearly enough space for all of them,' he reported. 'And there's hardly any water in their drinking trough.'

'I'm going to have a closer look,' Mandy decided. 'Walk on, Zebra.'

'Please don't!' Nick implored her. 'We can't risk making Mr Mackay suspicious.'

Mandy stopped. Nick was right. And going closer wouldn't prove anything more to her. It was clear, even from this distance, that the ponies were being badly treated. She turned Zebra round and rode him back to the top of the hill.

James held out his binoculars to her. 'Better to use these than risk bumping into Mr Mackay,' he said.

Mandy took them and slowly scanned the paddocks. When she came to the group of pregnant mares, she kept the glasses steady. Three of the ponies were looking in her direction. Mandy focused on their faces. 'Poor girls,' she murmured sympathetically, seeing a dullness in their eyes.

As Mandy pondered the miserable situation the ponies were in, a familiar feeling of anger rose up in her. 'Mr Mackay *can't* get away with this!' she said hotly.

Nick nodded. 'The trouble is, he *is* getting away with it because no one ever comes this way. We're probably the only ones who have seen what he's up to – apart from his staff. And they're probably too scared to say anything.'

'Well then, *we'll* just have to say something,' Mandy said defiantly. 'We must report him straightaway!' She pressed her legs into Zebra's sides and lightly pulled one of the reins. 'Let's go,' she said, turning Zebra for home.

'Hold on,' cried Nick, riding after her. 'We *can't* say anything yet. Otherwise we'll have to own up about Gandalf and I'm just not ready to do that now.'

Mandy halted Zebra and twisted round in her saddle. 'But the longer we wait, the worse it'll be for the ponies,' she protested.

'And who knows, someone might even find Gandalf,' put in James.

Nick sighed deeply and shook his head. 'No one will ever think of looking for Gandalf in that stable,' he said. 'But I agree we have to tell the police about Mr Mackay.' He wound the reins through his fingers. 'It's just that I want to make sure Gandalf's better first and . . .' he paused and looked at his watch, 'there are only two hours to go before the first part of Moss's assessment.'

Mandy appreciated Nick's dilemma. He had worked so hard preparing for this afternoon. Reporting Mr Mackay right now could upset everything. They could even end up missing the test altogether. 'I guess it won't make a huge difference if we wait until after the assessment,' she said.

Nick looked at her with relief. 'I'll tell Mum and the police as soon as Moss qualifies tomorrow,' he said.

As they rode away, Mandy turned and glanced back at the ponies. 'Hold on, all of you. Just for another day,' she called out to them in her mind. 'Help is on its way.'

Six

Moss was due to be put through her paces on another part of Ben Beag about half an hour from Kincraig. On the way there, Nick and his uncle told Mandy and James that quite a few dogs were being tested that day.

'Are they all trying for full rescue-dog status?' Mandy asked as they arrived at the field. The whole place was buzzing with activity. Several Border collies and German Shepherds, as well as a few Labradors and one or two cross-breeds padded alongside their handlers, who wore the same bright red jackets that Nick's Uncle John was wearing.

'Not all,' said Uncle John. 'Some will still be going for the lower grades.' He parked his Land-rover alongside several other vehicles. 'But they'll all have to locate the body.'

'The body?' echoed James, sounding appalled.

Mrs Russell laughed. '*Body* is probably a bit misleading,' she said. 'But that's what we call the volunteers who lie out for the dogs to find them.'

'I'm glad to hear that,' grinned James, opening the door and jumping out of the Land-rover. 'For a minute, I had a horrible picture in my mind.'

'You would!' Mandy teased. She turned to Uncle John. 'Do the handlers know where the people are lying?' she asked him.

'Only for Grade One,' said Uncle John, opening the back and putting a harness on Moss. 'For Grades Two, Three, Four and Five, only the assessors know where they are. And there's usually more than one body, as well as a number of other things that the dogs have to find.' He patted Moss's chest. 'OK, girl, out you get.'

Moss jumped down on to the grass and looked around eagerly, an alert expression on her intelligent face. She wagged her long bushy tail then, with an excited bark, glanced up at Nick.

Mandy could see she was raring to go. 'You can tell she's done this before,' she said, rubbing the top of Moss's head. 'She's so relaxed.'

'Yeah. She loves it all right,' said Nick. 'But it's still really nerve-wracking!'

'For you or me?' asked Uncle John with a twinkle in his eye.

Mandy looked at Uncle John. He seemed very composed. It was hard to imagine him being nervous.

They set off across the field to join the other teams. Halfway across, a sprightly middle-aged woman came up to them. A black Labrador ambled along next to her. 'Hello, everyone,' the woman said. 'Moss ready for her run?'

'As ready as she'll ever be,' smiled Mrs Russell. She introduced Mandy and James to the woman. 'This is Jill Peters,' she told them. 'She and her family come on day treks with us sometimes.' She bent down and patted the dog. 'How's Phoebe doing?'

'Beautifully!' said Mrs Peters. 'I'm confident we'll qualify this time round.'

While they were talking to Mrs Peters, two men came over to them. They were also wearing red jackets and were holding clipboards and stop watches. Mandy realised that they would be assessing Moss.

'Ready?' one of the men asked Uncle John.

Uncle John nodded confidently.

'Then let's get going,' said the judge. 'You'll be working the area with Jill and Phoebe as well as Robert Campbell and Spartacus.' He turned and beckoned to a tall man standing nearby with a strong-looking German shepherd.

The three teams spent a few minutes poring over a map and discussing their strategy, then called to the dogs and set off.

'This is it,' said Nick, whistling softly under his breath.

Keeping well back so as not to distract the dogs, Mandy, James, and Nick and his mum followed the team from the starting point at the bottom of a craggy hill.

Working from their maps, the teams fanned out across the hillside, then picked their way over the difficult ground. The dogs ranged ahead of their handlers who called out directions and encouragement to them from time to time.

Once, Uncle John stopped and put up his hand.

'What's he doing?' James asked Nick.

'Testing the wind direction,' Nick explained. 'It's best if the dogs work across the wind. You might even notice them doing some wind scenting.'

As he spoke, Moss stopped. She'd been following a track on the ground for quite a while but now she lifted her head and sniffed the air around her.

Uncle John waited, watching Moss carefully.

'She's definitely got wind of something,' said Mrs Russell. 'I hope it's the body.'

Moss seemed to be tasting the air. With a look of acute concentration, she twitched her sensitive nostrils then suddenly spun to her right and began scrambling purposefully up the hill.

'Yes!' said Nick excitedly. 'It looks like she's picked up the scent and the direction it's coming from.'

Moss scampered up the hill, leaping over boulders, stopping only to make sure the scent was still on the air. Sensing victory, her team of supporters continued after her, breathing heavily from the exertion of the climb.

After a while, Mandy looked back down the

slope. The field where they'd started out from was just a small patch of dark green far below. Above, the ground grew steeper and more craggy. Mandy remembered what Mrs Russell had said about Moss not being confident on slippery mountain slopes. She seems fine now, Mandy said to herself. That trek to Heathwylde the other night must have done her some good.

About a hundred metres ahead, Uncle John was working hard to keep up with Moss, who was ranging far ahead of him.

'I hope he doesn't lose sight of her,' Mandy said anxiously as they plodded on behind.

'That won't matter,' said Nick. 'When Moss finds the body she has to go back to Uncle John anyway, then lead him to it.'

Mandy looked across to where the two other teams were working their way up the hillside. Spartacus was also well ahead of his handler while Phoebe had found one of the hidden objects and was pointing it out to her handler. A rush of warmth flooded through Mandy. Dogs were such brilliant animals. And horses were just as important.

'You'd think Mr Mackay would appreciate his

horses a lot more than he seems to,' she muttered to herself.

'What's that, Mandy?' asked Mrs Russell.

Mandy swallowed. If she wasn't careful, she'd get them all into a lot of trouble. 'I was just thinking how tough Highland ponies are,' she said as she gingerly clambered over a mound of slippery rocks. Then, looking back up the hillside, she caught sight of Moss disappearing from view between two huge boulders.

Uncle John stopped briefly to tie a bootlace that had come undone, then continued up the slope. He hadn't gone very far when Moss reappeared from behind the boulders.

'She must have found something!' cried Nick.

Moss scrambled down the slope to Uncle John. But, just metres from him, she slipped on some loose stones and tumbled over on to her side. Mandy held her breath and shot a quick glance at Nick who was watching in dismay.

'Get up, Moss. Keep going,' Nick murmured.

Moss scrambled to her paws and looked around hesitantly. Nick sucked in his breath and looked across to the judges who were watching Moss with sombre faces. Then, to everyone's relief, Moss

started down the slope again, her ears pricked up and her tail held confidently behind her.

Nick breathed out loudly. 'Phew! That was a close call,' he said, his face breaking into a relieved smile.

Moss was panting heavily when she reached Uncle John. But she had enough breath left to bark urgently at him.

'Great! She's indicating,' said Nick.

'Indicating?' James echoed.

'That means she's telling her handler that she's found the body,' explained Mrs Russell.

Moss barked again. Uncle John quickly attached a long rope to her harness then the two of them powered their way up the hill.

'Come on,' called Nick. 'We can't miss this.'

To everyone's delight, Moss *had* found the body. A volunteer had been lying in a small ravine not far from the huge boulders.

'Well done!' the volunteer exclaimed, affectionately ruffling Moss's coat. 'You were really quick. I expected to be lying up here for hours.'

Nick was glowing with pride. 'Isn't she great!' he beamed.

'It looks like all your nocturnal practising has paid off, Nick,' said Mrs Russell. 'I've never seen Moss so confident.'

Nick cast Mandy and James a quick glance, then he turned to his uncle. 'I reckon she'll do it, don't you?'

Uncle John nodded. 'If she's this efficient in the next three runs, by tomorrow afternoon, she'll have her rescue-dog status.'

In high spirits, they went back down the mountain for a rest before Moss's second run. When the teams set off again, everyone was feeling very optimistic. But it wasn't long into the search when Moss hesitated while picking her way down a steep slope. Mandy tensed, wondering if Moss's earlier fall had made her more nervous than before.

'Go on, Moss,' Nick implored under his breath as he watched his uncle urging her on. 'You've been down much steeper hills than that.'

Moss dug in her heels then tried to back up the slope again.

Nick groaned. 'No! She *can't* fail now.'

And then, as if his quiet pleas had reached her, Moss tentatively began to edge her way down the hill again.

Mandy felt the tension drain out of her. 'For a minute there, I thought it was all over,' she said.

The second run proved to be more challenging than the first. The volunteer was hiding in a deep gully on the other side of a swiftly flowing river. The rescue teams had to negotiate their way down the slippery river banks, and then cross the river by means of some large boulders that acted as stepping stones. Another complication was that the wind had dropped, which made it difficult for the dogs to pick up any wind-borne scent. This meant that Moss had to rely mainly on tracking the scent on the ground.

The exercise took over an hour but at last Moss and Uncle John succeeded in locating the body.

'Just the one slip-up going down that slope,' said Uncle John when they were heading back down to the field. 'We'll have to hope the judges weren't put off by her hesitation.'

'They can't be,' said Nick, rewarding Moss for her good performance with a tasty treat. 'She did everything else perfectly.'

Mandy smoothed the collie's thick coat. 'Well done, girl,' she said. 'And tomorrow, you're going to do even better.'

* * *

That night, Mandy, James and Nick slipped out of the house after dinner to visit Gandalf. They took more pony nuts with them and another poultice, just in case the stallion's foot needed more attention. They also managed to take a fork and a broom so that they could clean out the stable.

Gandalf was glad to see them. He snorted loudly when they opened the door then sniffed at the bag of pony nuts that Mandy was carrying.

Mandy gave him a handful. 'Poor hungry boy,' she said soothingly to him as she stroked his neck. 'You need to be back out in the open so that you can graze freely, don't you?' She turned to Nick. 'Let's walk him outside and see if his foot's any better.'

Nick attached a rope to Gandalf's headcollar and they led him outside. The stallion immediately dropped his head and began nibbling the coarse grass.

Nick let him graze for a few minutes then walked him around in a circle.

'He's still a bit lame,' said Mandy, noticing that he was favouring his injured foot.

'All the more reason he can't go back to Heathwylde yet,' said Nick grimly.

Mandy gave James a fleeting look. Nick was still so intent on hiding the stallion. She hoped he would keep his promise to tell his mum about Gandalf as soon as Moss's assessment was over.

They left Gandalf to graze while they mucked out the stable. When it was clean, James fetched some fresh water then Nick led the stallion back inside.

After his taste of freedom, Gandalf seemed reluctant to go back into the stable. He stood stubbornly rooted to the spot when Nick tried to lead him in again.

'We're really sorry,' Mandy murmured to the pony, luring him forward with some more pony nuts.

Gandalf stared at her with big, sad eyes then walked slowly after her.

'But it won't be for much longer,' she continued, patting his warm, muscular neck as he entered the stable next to her. 'Just until tomorrow, then . . .' Mandy couldn't go on. What *would* happen tomorrow when they reported everything to the police? Would everything be all right?

Mandy glanced at Nick who was leaning against the doorframe. If Mr Mackay *did* get away with everything, then Nick would be in big trouble.

They applied the fresh poultice and this time Gandalf stood quietly while they treated him. 'I think he trusts us now,' Mandy said, tying the new plastic bag on to his foot.

When they had finished, they gave Gandalf the rest of the pony nuts then closed the rickety stable door and headed back to the house.

That night, Mandy's dreams were a confused kaleidoscope of horses, dogs and red-jacketed people clambering up mountains and in and out of stables. Images of an angry Mr Mackay kept appearing too. The dreams faded when Mandy woke up in the morning – but she couldn't stop thinking about them.

The images stayed with her until they arrived at the field later that morning for Moss's next two runs. As the collie started out on her rescue mission, Mandy managed to shake off the nightmare and concentrate on the important job ahead. 'Good luck, Moss,' she said, giving her an encouraging pat.

Moss and Uncle John set off enthusiastically,

their supporters some distance behind them. After a while, Moss picked up an airborne scent and began tracking it across the mountainside. The scent trailed to a slippery slope of scree that fell steeply down to a narrow river valley. Cautiously, Moss took a few steps down the slope then, just when it seemed she was gaining in confidence, she slipped.

'It's all right,' Mandy heard Uncle John call out to Moss as she steadied herself by turning sideways and planting her paws firmly on the ground. 'Go on, girl. You're fine.'

But Moss didn't think it was all right. She stood motionless, staring nervously down the slope. And then, to Nick's dismay, she began sidling back up the hill.

'No!' cried Nick. 'She *must* go on.'

Uncle John tried to urge her forward again but Moss had made up her mind. She refused point blank to go on. She reached the top of the slope then doubled-back to Uncle John and sat in front of him, sheepishly sweeping the ground with her plumy tail.

Nick was devastated. 'It's all over,' he said, his voice catching in his throat as he fought back tears.

One of the judges went over to speak to Uncle John as he and Moss returned to the group. 'She shows a lot of promise,' Mandy heard the man say, 'but you know we can't pass a dog that refuses to follow the scent.'

Nick had also overheard the judge's verdict. He swallowed hard. 'Now we'll have to wait another six months for the next assessment weekend,' he said, looking away as he wiped his eyes. 'I can't believe it. She was so good on the slopes yesterday.'

Deeply disappointed, they all turned back down the mountain and headed for the field where Uncle John's car was parked. It was a very sombre group that set off for home a short while later.

'Mum's going to be just as upset,' said Nick sadly as they turned on to the road leading to Kincraig.

Mrs Russell had stayed at home that day because she was hoping for a response to an advert she'd placed in the newspaper.

'I'll break the news to her,' said Uncle John kindly.

But it was an angry-looking Mrs Russell who broke her news to them first. She and Morag were in the field – with just one of the ponies. 'I'm so glad you're home,' she said when she saw them all coming over to her. 'We've had a terrible time this afternoon.'

'Where are all the ponies?' asked Nick, looking round in amazement.

'That's a good question,' said Mrs Russell, coming out of the field and closing the gate behind her. 'You're going to have to help me round them up. They're all over the hillside.'

'How did that happen?' asked James.

'They followed a trek that came across our land soon after Clare and Rachel left today,' answered Mrs Russell. 'They must have been from Heathwylde. The grooms who were riding them must be new – they clearly have no idea where they can and can't ride. They went right through our field and left the gates open.' She folded her arms and shook her head. 'I wish people would be more considerate.'

James nudged Mandy then silently mouthed, 'Heathwylde!'

Mandy nodded grimly. Given what she knew of Mr Mackay, nothing about his operation surprised her at all. She went with Nick to fetch some leading reins from the stable yard. 'I thought you were going to tell your mum about Gandalf now,' she reminded him.

'I will,' he said. 'Just as soon as we've checked on him.'

Mandy looked sideways at Nick. Surely he wasn't backing out of his promise? But she decided not to press the point any further. Nick was obviously still upset about Moss. He probably needed a bit more time before he could bring himself to speak to his mum about Gandalf. Also, they had to find the ponies before they could do anything else.

They took the lead ropes out to Morag and James, then the four of them started bringing in the horses from the hillside. Luckily, none of them had strayed very far, and they all seemed happy to be caught.

'It looks like we're in for some bad weather,' said Morag when they were leading the last three ponies back to the paddock. She looked up at the heavy black clouds that were gathering above the mountain. Swathes of grey mist were also collecting on the slopes. 'I hope it holds off for a while. I'm meeting some of my friends in Aberford this evening.'

'It had *better* hold off,' Nick said firmly and

Mandy knew he was thinking about how awkward it would be for them if they had to go up to Gandalf in the rain.

Back in the house, Uncle John had told Mrs Russell about Moss's failure. But she wasn't as disappointed as Nick had predicted. Instead, she comforted Nick by reminding him that Moss was still very young. 'Another six months will make all the difference to her confidence,' she told him.

Uncle John left shortly after supper, giving Morag a lift down the mountain.

'Will you three clear up in the kitchen and feed the dogs for me?' Mrs Russell asked Mandy, James and Nick. 'I have to catch up on some office work.'

'That's a nuisance,' Nick whispered to Mandy and James as they carried through the supper dishes. 'I was hoping we'd be able to go and see Gandalf before the weather gets any worse.'

By the time they did manage to slip out, the wind was gusting strongly and dense mist was rolling down into the valleys.

'No, Moss. Stay!' said Nick seeing her follow them out of the house.

But Moss ignored his command and padded on behind them.

'Oh well. I guess you need the practice,' said Nick, changing his mind and patting his thigh to encourage her to keep up with him.

The worsening weather made their walk up to the stable much slower. Dark clouds gathering overhead blocked out the evening light, making it hard for them to see their way clearly.

James switched on his torch but the beam made very little difference. 'We'll just have to *feel* our way up,' he said.

They leaned forward into the driving wind and forced their way onwards. Finally they clambered up the last slope to the field. In the gloom, they could just make out the shape of the stable ahead of them.

'I don't think we'd better stay too long,' said Nick as they ran across the field. 'We'll just check . . .'

A creaking noise interrupted him.

And then, as Mandy peered through the gloom she saw something that made her heart skip a beat. 'Look!' she gasped, pointing at the stable.

The door was wide open. It swung back and forth in the wind, the creaking sound acting like a siren telling Mandy one thing. Gandalf had gone!

Seven

Mandy charged through the gaping door with James and Nick hard on her heels. The only signs that a pony had been there were the half-full bucket of water and the soiled straw on the floor.

'I don't believe it,' Mandy groaned in despair. 'Mr Mackay must have found him and taken him back.'

Nick was staring out of the door. He turned and shook his head. Even in the half-light, Mandy could see that the colour had drained out of his face. 'I don't think so,' he said slowly. 'If he'd found Gandalf, we'd have heard all about it by now. He'd have made a huge fuss trying to find out who'd brought him here.'

'I guess that makes sense,' said Mandy, watching Moss who was sniffing around the stable. 'But if Mr Mackay didn't steal him back, then who did?'

James was shining his torch around the stable. 'Maybe no one,' he said.

Mandy frowned at him. 'What do you mean?'

'Gandalf might have got out by himself,' he answered. 'Look at this.'

He pointed the torch beam at the doorframe. Mandy and Nick looked closer. The wood was old and warped. But it was also badly splintered – right where the bolt from the door would normally slide across.

'That's it,' said Nick, running his hand up and down the shattered frame. 'Gandalf must have kicked the door open and escaped.'

'But why?' Mandy frowned. 'After all, he was still lame last night. Surely he wouldn't *want* to go anywhere?'

'Not unless something made him really desperate to get out,' said Nick. He chewed his thumbnail thoughtfully. 'And I bet I know what that was. Those ponies from Heathwylde.'

'The ones that came through Kincraig today?' asked James, putting his torch back in his pocket.

'Uh-huh,' said Nick. 'I bet they came up the back way that goes past this field – the same path we were on the other day. Gandalf must have heard them and barged his way out.'

'But that means he probably *is* back at Heathwylde,' said Mandy. 'He'd have followed them home.'

Nick went outside. 'I hope not,' he said grimly. He looked up to where the ponies would have passed by. 'He might have tried, but they'd have had a head start on him. And don't forget, his foot injury would have slowed him down a lot, especially if he made it worse again by kicking at the door.'

Mandy winced. 'And just when it was looking a lot better,' she said as she and James followed Nick outside.

A strong gust of wind slammed the door hard against the outside wall of the stable. Mandy pictured Gandalf wandering about somewhere in the mountains. Even though he was a hardy Highland pony, he was in no condition to be out there all alone. Anything could happen to him.

The wind drove heavy drops of rain into Mandy's face. She zipped up her jacket and pulled up the hood. They had no option. 'We've got to find him,' she said, shoving her hands deep into her pockets.

'But we don't even know where to begin,' James pointed out, waving his arm in a sweeping gesture that took in the entire mountain and the valleys below. 'Just say Gandalf *didn't* go after the other ponies. He could be anywhere! We'd need to be expert trackers to find him – especially in this weather.'

Mandy was about to agree. 'I guess . . .' she began, then stopped abruptly as she saw Moss sniffing the stable door. 'But there *is* an expert tracker amongst us,' she cried. 'Moss! She'll find Gandalf. Won't you, girl?'

Hearing her name, Moss trotted over to Mandy and pushed her long nose against her hand.

'You might be a bit nervous when it comes to steep slopes,' said Mandy, smoothing Moss's head. 'But there's nothing wrong with your tracking ability.' She turned to Nick. 'What do you think?'

'It's a great idea,' replied Nick, his face alive with enthusiasm. 'Let's get going now!' He helped

Moss to pick up Gandalf's scent by encouraging her to sniff the straw on the ground. 'Find, Moss. Find!' he said.

With her tail wagging, Moss put her nose to the ground and set off, tracing the invisible track that Gandalf had left.

They followed Moss across the field, then clambered up a rocky slope and finally on to the contour path that wound its way around the mountain. Moss scampered along the path for a few hundred metres, then stopped suddenly and lifted her head. She sniffed the air delicately.

Mandy, James and Nick waited silently. Moss continued to taste the air that came pouring down the mountain on the blustery wind. Then with a decisive flick of her tail, she started off once more. But instead of following the path again, she left it and headed straight up the mountain.

'Gandalf *has* headed back to Heathwylde,' Nick confirmed as they stumbled along behind Moss. 'This is the shortest – and roughest – way there.'

'Which means he must have reached the stud by now,' said James despondently.

'Well, we're not giving up until we know for sure,' Mandy insisted. She paused to push a damp strand of hair out of her eyes, then leaned forward again and pressed on up the slope behind Moss.

With the rain falling steadily, the ground was very slippery beneath them. But this was not enough to deter them from their chase. Even Moss took it in her stride, moving steadily over the tricky terrain.

Nick paused and watched breathlessly as his dog skidded on some loose scree, but she quickly regained her footing and went on confidently. 'Why wasn't she like this in the assessment?' he agonised out loud.

The airborne scent led Moss over the mountain and down the other side. The descent turned out to be even more taxing than the way up and Mandy found herself sliding almost helplessly down the steep hill. 'If we keep this up, we'll be at the bottom in a flash,' she gasped, grabbing a rock to steady herself for the umpteenth time. And then, as she peered down the mountain, she saw some lights twinkling not far away. 'Hey! I think we're nearly there,' she called to Nick and James.

The steep hillside gradually gave way to more level ground and before long they were barely fifty metres from the stud farm. Only a deep ditch came between them and the nearest paddock where a group of ponies huddled together, trying to shelter from the squall.

Mandy looked hard but she couldn't see Gandalf among them. 'Now what?' she asked, glancing at Nick. He seemed deep in thought. Surely he wasn't thinking of going in and stealing Gandalf back again? He'd got away with it once but his luck probably wouldn't hold out a second time. And besides, they needed to find a much more permanent solution to the problem.

A few metres away, Moss was still on the stallion's trail. She nosed her way along the edge of the ditch, her eyes and ears alert. As Mandy watched her working, the graceful collie froze. She leaned forward and stared into the narrow gully. Then she whirled round and raced back to Nick, barking urgently at him.

'She's found him!' cried Nick, charging along the bank behind her.

Mandy and James caught up with them just when Moss stopped again. James pulled out his torch and shone it down into the ditch. A pair of bright eyes shone back at them. It was Gandalf! He hadn't made it back to the stud after all. He was lying on one side, trapped at the bottom of the gully. As Mandy looked down at him in horror, he began to thrash about wildly, trying to get up.

'Oh, no!' Mandy cried. 'We've got to get him out of there.'

She scrambled down the steep walls of the ditch and carefully approached Gandalf, keeping well out of reach of his flailing hooves. The stallion was lying with his legs sticking out stiffly. Mandy guessed that he must have been trying to cross over into the field to the other ponies but, hampered by his bad hoof, had slipped into the ditch.

'Poor Gandalf,' Mandy murmured in a soothing voice, making her way round to his head. She stroked his shoulder, hoping desperately that he wasn't badly injured.

Nick jumped down next to her and called back up to James to keep Moss with him. 'She might get hurt down here,' he said. He turned his attention back to Gandalf. 'He's stuck fast, and exhausted too. I wonder how long he's been down here?'

'Too long,' Mandy replied. 'We have to get him out.'

'We can't,' said Nick. 'Not without help.'

'Then I'll go for help,' James called down. 'Moss and I will go back to Kincraig to tell your mum, Nick. She'll know what to do.' And without another word, he disappeared from the top of the bank.

It was dark and damp in the ditch. Mandy wished they'd asked James to leave his torch. But going back over the mountain in this weather, he'll need it more than we do, she reasoned. She wondered what Mrs Russell would say when she found out what had been going on. Would she be on their side or would she be furious that Nick had caused trouble with their neighbour? Mandy turned to Nick. 'How long do you think it'll be before your mum gets here?'

'Allowing an hour or so for James to get home, at least an hour and a half – maybe even two,' answered Nick.

Two hours! Could Gandalf wait that long? The stallion seemed to have given up because he had stopped struggling and was now lying quite still. Mandy rubbed his chest gently. She stopped and listened. He seemed to be breathing rather erratically. She felt his rib cage. It rose only slightly as he breathed in. 'He's having trouble breathing,' she told Nick anxiously.

Nick listened. 'You're right,' he said. 'It's probably because of the way he's lying.'

'Then we can't wait for your mum to get here,' Mandy decided. 'That'll be too late. 'We've got to get help *now*.'

'You know what that means, don't you?' said Nick solemnly.

Mandy nodded. 'Mr Mackay. He's the nearest person.' She hesitated for only the briefest moment, then began hauling her way out of the ditch. 'I'll go and fetch him,' she said.

'Be careful, Mandy,' called Nick.

'I will,' she shouted over the howling gale as she clapped her hands together to beat off the mud.

She ran past the paddocks, stumbling over the rough ground a few times before she finally reached the main house. 'Mr Mackay,' she called out at the top of her voice as she banged urgently on the front door. 'Come quickly. There's an emergency.'

A few moments later, the heavy oak door swung open and Mandy was face-to-face with the surly man once more. 'There's a pony in trouble,' she blurted out. 'Please come and help him.'

'What pony?' snapped Mr Mackay.

'Gandalf's Secret,' Mandy told him. 'He was on his way back here and . . .'

Mr Mackay's eyes grew wide. He interrupted Mandy. 'Gandalf's Secret? Is that what you said?'

Mandy nodded and went on quickly. 'Yes. He's stuck in a ditch. Nick and I think . . .'

But Mr Mackay cut her off again. 'So Gandalf's Secret was on his way back here,' he said, ignoring what Mandy had told him about the stallion being trapped. 'Where exactly was he coming back from?'

'From the old stable on the other side of the mountain,' Mandy said. 'But we can't worry about all that now,' she begged him. 'We've got to get him out of the ditch.'

Mr Mackay put his hands on his hips and glared angrily at Mandy. 'Are you saying that you and your friend stole my horse?' he demanded.

'But Nick didn't mean any harm,' Mandy cried, realising too late that she'd given Nick away. 'He was only trying to help Gandalf.'

'*Help* one of *my* horses!' said Mr Mackay angrily. 'Who does that young upstart think he is? Does his mother know what he's been up to?'

Mandy shook her head. 'Not yet. But James . . .'

Mr Mackay impatiently cut in again. 'Well, I think it's time Mrs Russell found out!' He turned and marched across the hallway towards the telephone.

Mandy felt a knot of frustration in the pit of her stomach. Instead of getting help for Gandalf, she had only made things worse. Without thinking, she ran in after Mr Mackay, her boots leaving a trail of mud on the floor behind her.

'Please don't,' she begged. 'There isn't time for this. We must help Gandalf.'

Mr Mackay was flipping through the telephone directory. 'I'll look at the horse just as soon as I've spoken to Mrs Russell,' he said, lifting the receiver. He dialled the number and a few seconds later he was talking to Nick's mum. 'Angus Mackay here,' he told her. 'You ought to know that I've got one of your guests here. She tells me that it was your son who removed my horse.'

There was a pause while Mrs Russell said something in reply, then Mr Mackay said, 'Yes, his friend is standing right here with me. She told me exactly what he's been up to. She can tell you about it herself.'

He handed the receiver to Mandy. At the other end of the line, Mrs Russell sounded very confused. 'Mandy? What on earth is going on? Did Nick really steal Gandalf?'

Mandy took a deep breath. 'He wasn't actually *stealing* him,' she explained. 'But he *did* take Gandalf away because he was in a bad way. And now Gandalf's stuck in a ditch. We have to get him out.'

'I'll be there as soon as I can,' said Mrs Russell.

'And tell Nick to stay out of any more trouble!' She hung up and Mandy put the receiver back on its cradle.

'Mrs Russell's coming over,' she told Mr Mackay.

'Good. And in the meantime, you can show me where my horse is,' said Mr Mackay. He took an oilskin jacket off a coat rack then pulled on a pair of boots. 'This is all I need on such a filthy night,' he grumbled, reaching for a torch on a shelf behind the door.

In silence, Mandy led him out to the ditch. She wondered what Mr Mackay would do when he saw Gandalf. Would he really be uncaring enough to wait until morning before he did anything?

As they approached the ditch, Mandy called out to Nick. 'Mr Mackay's come to see what's happened.'

Mr Mackay shone his torch into the ditch, lighting up an anxious-looking Nick and the exhausted Gandalf. 'How on earth did this happen?' he said angrily. Then, without waiting for an answer, he scrambled down into the ditch to take a closer look at his horse.

Gandalf was lying quite still. Mr Mackay quickly sized up the situation. 'He's stuck, all right,' he said grimly. 'And he might even be seriously injured.' He glared at Nick. 'You're in big trouble, lad. But right now, I need to sort the horse out. I'll fetch some of my grooms to help me.' He climbed out of the ditch and strode away towards the farm buildings.

As Mandy watched him go, a sudden squall of rain pelted her in the face. She pulled her hood up over her head then climbed back down to Nick and Gandalf.

'I guess Mr Mackay will report me to the police,' said Nick miserably.

Mandy nodded sympathetically. 'If only Gandalf hadn't fallen into the ditch!' She patted Gandalf's shoulder. The pony lifted his head and looked at her sadly then made another weak attempt to get up.

'It's all right,' Mandy said in a soothing voice. Then turning back to Nick she added, 'But at least Mr Mackay's gone for help. It won't be long before Gandalf's out of here.'

Eight

Mr Mackay returned a short while later with two grooms. They stood at the top of the bank and discussed how to get the stallion out of the ditch.

'I suppose we could pull him out with a tractor,' said one of the men. He sounded rather uncertain, as if he wasn't used to helping stuck horses.

Mandy winced. Surely there was a gentler approach? 'Can't we try to heave him up on to his feet?' she suggested. 'Then he might be able to get out by himself.'

'That won't work,' responded Mr Mackay gruffly. 'Especially if he's hurt a leg.'

'But in that case we need to be all the more careful,' Mandy protested. 'Why don't we try using a bale of straw to support him? Maybe he can get himself out.'

Mr Mackay frowned, then nodded at his grooms. One of them jogged off and fetched a bale of straw from the stables, then dragged it down into the ditch.

'We'll push him up gradually and use the straw bale to prop him up,' said Nick. Still looking doubtful, the grooms slithered into the ditch beside Mandy and Nick and got ready to help. One of the grooms patted Gandalf rather awkwardly on his flank, and Mandy realised the grooms didn't mean any harm to the ponies; they just weren't used to dealing with them.

While the grooms prepared to begin lifting Gandalf, Mr Mackay looked on from the top of the ditch. He could help, Mandy thought indignantly.

Mandy and Nick had just positioned themselves behind the straw bale when they heard Mr Mackay saying, 'Ah. There's Mrs Russell now. And who's that with her?' He paused then added, 'It looks like Jane Fraser.'

Mandy was wondering who Jane Fraser was

when Mrs Russell appeared at the top of the ditch and looked down at them. Next to her was a dark-haired young woman.

'Are you two all right?' asked Mrs Russell anxiously.

'We're fine,' Mandy said. 'But Gandalf isn't.'

The grooms were about to start heaving the stallion up when Jane Fraser said suddenly, 'Wait. Let me see to him first,' and started to work her way down the slimy bank.

Mandy's heart leaped. Miss Fraser was carrying a big black bag – exactly like the one her mum and dad used. She must be a vet!

Mr Mackay folded his arms. 'I hope you're paying for the vet,' he said to Mrs Russell, 'seeing as this is all your son's fault.'

'I'm quite happy to pay the bill but I think Nick should at least be given the chance to explain things before we decide whose fault it is,' answered Mrs Russell. 'But that can wait until after Jane has seen to the pony.'

At the bottom of the ditch, Miss Fraser switched on a torch and examined Gandalf carefully.

'Do you think he's hurt his legs?' Mrs Russell asked.

'It's hard to say,' replied the vet. She took out a small glass phial and a syringe. 'I'll give him a painkilling injection first. As soon as that kicks in, we'll be able to start moving him. I'll be able to tell you more when he's on his feet.'

Miss Fraser injected the medication into Gandalf's shoulder muscle then waited while it took effect.

'Perhaps now is as good a time as any for you to tell us exactly what you've been up to, Nick,' said Mrs Russell, sitting on her haunches and peering down at Nick.

Quickly Nick started to explain why he had taken Gandalf away from Heathwylde.

Mr Mackay listened with a stern expression on his face then, when Nick had finished, said angrily, 'What happens on this farm is none of your business. My horses are just fine. You had no right to interfere with any of them!'

Nick shook his head slowly. 'They aren't fine,' he insisted quietly. He looked back up at his mum. 'I was going to tell you everything tonight, Mum,' he said. 'Honestly. But Gandalf escaped and we just *had* to find him first.'

Mrs Russell smiled at him. 'You've got a good

heart, Nick,' she said softly. 'And do you know what?'

'What?' asked Nick.

'At your age, and in a similar situation, I'd probably have done exactly the same thing,' she admitted.

Jane Fraser shut her bag and passed it up the bank to Mrs Russell. 'You say the ponies aren't fine,' she prompted Nick.

'That's right,' Nick confirmed. 'Mandy, James and I saw them yesterday when we rode past here. James had his binoculars so we had a really good look at them.'

The mention of James made Mandy wonder where he was. With all that had been going on, she'd almost forgotten about him. 'James went back with Moss to tell you what had happened,' she told Mrs Russell. 'Didn't you see them?'

'No. I haven't seen any of you since suppertime,' answered Mrs Russell.

'He probably arrived after you left,' Mandy reasoned. 'So he won't know that you've come over here. I guess he's wondering what to do now.'

'Well, if he has any sense, he'll stay where he is,' said Mrs Russell, squinting her eyes against the rain as she looked up at the heavy clouds scudding across the sky. 'This storm won't blow over tonight.'

Miss Fraser patted Gandalf's neck. 'Right then, boy. You've been here long enough. Let's get you out of here.'

Straining under the weight of the exhausted pony, the two grooms and Miss Fraser slowly started pushing Gandalf up. Mrs Russell clambered down to help them and eventually Gandalf's side was clear of the ground. Quickly Mandy and Nick slid the straw bale beneath him to stop him from falling back down again. Miss Fraser then went round and carefully released the stallion's legs from their stiff position. 'The next step is to move him on to his chest,' she said.

They began to heave him forward. Gandalf seemed bewildered by all the activity around him. The whites of his eyes flashed and his nostrils flared as he tried to make sense of what was happening. He struggled and kicked out, then lurched forward. This was just the help his rescuers needed, for he managed to push himself on to his chest. Then, feeling his back hooves strike the ground beneath him, a look of relief flooded his face and he began to scrabble at the ground with his forelegs.

'Just one big push and you're there, Gandalf,' Mandy encouraged him.

Everyone stood back and the tired pony paused for a moment's rest. Then, with a mighty effort, he pushed himself up on to all four legs.

'Great!' Mandy cried. 'You've done it, Gandalf.'

'Now if you two lead him up the bank from the front,' said Miss Fraser to Mandy and Nick, 'we'll join hands behind his tail and push him from behind.'

Mandy and Nick each took hold of one side of Gandalf's headcollar and started to pull. But the stallion had decided it was time to help himself. He suddenly surged forward and with a few nimble movements scrambled up to the top of the bank.

'That's a boy, Gandalf!' cried Nick, climbing up after him.

Mr Mackay had watched the entire proceedings with his arms folded stiffly across his chest. Then, as Gandalf reached the top of the bank, Mr Mackay made a grab for him. But Gandalf shied away quickly and trotted towards the ponies in the nearby paddock, his gait showing that he was still lame.

Miss Fraser went after him. 'I'll just check that hoof,' she said. But as she neared the railings, she stopped and looked at the ponies who were leaning over to sniff at Gandalf. She flashed her torch into the paddock.

'What's wrong?' Mandy asked, going over to her.

'Nick was right about the horses being neglected. This paddock's terribly crowded,' Miss Fraser said. She shone the torch at the water trough. 'And that water is filthy.'

She called to Mr Mackay who was talking earnestly to the three grooms. 'Could I have a word with you, Mr Mackay?'

Mr Mackay came over to her. 'What's the problem?' he asked.

'I'm not happy about the state of these horses,' Miss Fraser told him.

'And I'm not happy about all this interference in my affairs,' Mr Mackay replied curtly. 'I want you all to leave. Now.'

Miss Fraser shook her head. 'We're not doing that in a hurry,' she replied. 'I'm going to see to Gandalf's foot, then I want you to join me while I inspect the rest of the ponies. After that, I'll be phoning the SSPCA to report on the conditions here.'

Mandy glanced at Mr Mackay. He looked furious. But there was nothing he could do now to cover up what had been going on at Heathwylde.

'Let's take Gandalf to the stables where I can have a good look at him in the light,' said Miss Fraser.

Mandy and Nick led Gandalf across to the stable yard. Mrs Russell and Miss Fraser walked behind them, flanked by a grim-faced Mr Mackay and his grooms.

In the yard, Nick and Mandy helped to hold Gandalf and support his leg while Miss Fraser removed the dressing. She examined his hoof closely. 'It's not looking too bad,' she announced. 'Even after his long trek tonight.' She looked up at Nick and Mandy. 'Your treatment was spot on. I'm very impressed – particularly as it's not always easy to handle a stallion in pain.' She opened her treatment bag and took out a fresh poultice. 'I'll replace the dressing, but what Gandalf needs most of all is to be fed and watered and put inside where he can have some rest. Will you two see to him while the rest of us check on the other horses?'

'Of course,' said Nick happily.

Mandy and Nick led Gandalf over to a loose box. Mandy looked inside. 'We'll have to clean it out first,' she said. 'It's full of old straw.'

While Gandalf watched curiously from the yard, Mandy and Nick swept out the stable then spread clean straw on the floor. When they'd finished, Nick went to fetch a bucket of clean water while Mandy led Gandalf inside.

The pony looked around at his clean surroundings and snorted appreciatively. 'That's better, isn't it?' Mandy said, giving him a handful of the pony nuts which they'd carried with them all the way over the mountain. She tipped the rest into a bucket. 'Just as well we didn't give up on you and leave these in that old stable,' she said with a smile.

By the time Gandalf was settled in his clean stall, Jane Fraser and the others had finished their tour of the paddocks. Mandy and Nick caught up with them as they went over to the house. No one was speaking but Mandy saw very serious expressions on all their faces.

Inside, Miss Fraser went straight to the telephone and called the Scottish Society for the Prevention of Cruelty to Animals. She explained what she'd seen at the farm and asked for an official to come out the next day. 'I'll come back to speak to the inspector in the morning but in the meantime, we'll do what we can to make the ponies comfortable for the night,' she said.

Mandy couldn't help looking at Mr Mackay. He

was pacing back and forth in the hallway, looking very agitated.

Miss Fraser put the phone down and turned to Mr Mackay. 'I think it's best if you stay away from the ponies until the SSPCA has spoken to you,' she said. 'But I'll need the help of your staff. There's a lot to do tonight.'

Mr Mackay nodded briefly then walked over to the stairs muttering, 'I'll be talking to my lawyer about this in the morning.'

'I'm not sure he'll be able to do much for you,' said Miss Fraser. She went to the door. 'Right. Let's get started, everyone. We're going to have to put the pregnant mares into stables, spread the rest of the ponies more evenly around the paddocks and make sure they all have clean water and enough to eat for the night.' She frowned for a moment at Mr Mackay's grooms. 'Do you think you two can manage that, if I tell you what to do?'

The grooms nodded vigorously. 'Oh yes,' said one of them. 'We'll definitely give you a hand.'

They had almost reached the paddocks when Mrs Russell stopped. 'Perhaps I ought to phone James,' she said. 'I'm sure he'll be wondering where we all are.'

But just as she turned to go back to the house, Mandy heard a distinct bark. It was coming from the direction of the ditch where Gandalf had been lying. 'Moss!' she said, recognising the collie's bark.

Miss Fraser pointed her torch towards the ditch. The narrow beam lit up the edge of the bank – and Moss's brown and white face.

'Moss! What's the matter?' cried Nick, running over to meet her.

Moss replied with an urgent, high-pitched bark – one that Mandy now understood only too well. Moss was indicating in exactly the same way as she had when she'd found the body in the mountains the day before.

'James!' Mandy gasped. 'Something must have happened to James!'

Nine

There was no doubt in Mandy's mind that Moss had come to fetch them. The collie spun round and started heading back towards the mountains.

'Let's go,' cried Nick, charging after her with Mandy and his mum hot on his heels.

'I'll come with you,' Miss Fraser said, calling to the grooms to begin fetching in the mares. 'Just get them in the dry and I'll examine them later,' she instructed, running after the others as they dashed across the field.

They scrambled into the ditch, clambered up the bank on the far side and were soon working their way up into the mountains. All around them, forks of lightning ripped through the sky while the menacing rumble of thunder added to the urgency that was building up within Mandy. What's happened to James? she agonised to herself over and over again.

They crested a steep hill then started picking their way down the other side. The ground felt greasy beneath them. They skidded and slid down the slope, grabbing on to rocks and gorse shrubs for support whenever they could. Without Miss Fraser's torch lighting their way, the going would have been almost impossibly treacherous.

Ahead of them, Moss scrambled fearlessly across the loose scree that littered the mountainside. Although she was desperately worried about James, Mandy couldn't help being impressed. She's so much more confident than she was for her assessment this afternoon, she told herself. She's like a different dog!

'We're almost back at the stable,' puffed Nick when at last they reached the bottom of the hill.

They passed close by some old sheep-pen hurdles Mandy remembered seeing earlier that evening, and before long came to the wide field where the stable stood, its door still swinging back and forth in the wind. Moss hurtled towards it and Mandy thought for a moment that they'd find James inside. But Moss continued straight past the shack then disappeared over the edge of the field where the land plunged down to the narrow river valley.

Mandy knew this part of Ben Beag very well by now. They'd come this way several times in the past few days. *We're really close to Kincraig*, she told herself. Her hopes began to rise. James might have made it back to the centre after all. She turned to Nick. 'Perhaps James was worried when he found no one at home,' she suggested hopefully. 'Maybe he sent Moss back for us.'

But Mandy's words tailed away as Moss jumped on to a big flat rock that jutted out above a narrow cleft and started to bark sharply. Then she whirled round and ran back to Nick, still barking as if her life depended on it.

'James must be down there,' Mandy cried. She paused and took a deep breath, afraid of what they were going to find.

And then, from down within the crevice came a sound that flooded Mandy with relief.

'Help! I'm down here!' came James's voice.

'Thank goodness!' cried Mrs Russell. 'At least he's conscious.'

They knelt on the rock and looked down. A metre or two below them was James's huddled-up figure. Miss Fraser shone her torch into the narrow cleft, showing him clearly. His foot seemed to be wedged between two big boulders.

'Are you all right?' Mandy called down, her heart pounding in her chest.

'I don't know,' came the reply. 'I slipped on some loose stones and fell down here. My ankle's hurting like mad and I can't move.'

'Don't worry,' Mandy called reassuringly. 'We know exactly what to do. We've done a rescue like this once already tonight!'

'You mean Gandalf's OK?' James responded, his voice charged with pleasure.

'He's going to be fine,' Nick told him.

'Brilliant!' cried James happily.

Mandy had to chuckle. Good old James! Even though he was in real trouble, he was still more concerned for animals than for himself. No wonder he was her best friend!

While Mrs Russell and Miss Fraser went down

to James, Mandy and Nick climbed back up to the field to fetch a sheep-pen hurdle to use as a stretcher. Since it was flat and shaped like a door, the hurdle would be perfect for the job.

Gingerly they carried it down to the bottom of the crevice, where Mrs Russell and Miss Fraser were already seeing to James.

'It looks like you've sprained your ankle,' Miss Fraser told James, feeling his foot. 'So it's nothing too serious. But you won't be able to walk on it for a while. We'll definitely have to stretcher you out of here.'

There was very little room for them to manoeuvre in the narrow cleft, but eventually they managed to free James from between the rocks and lift him on to the makeshift stretcher. Painstakingly, they edged him out of his rocky prison and back on to the path.

'Thanks, everyone,' said James. 'But especially you, Moss.' He reached out and patted her head as she padded along protectively at his side. Then he looked up at Mandy. 'She stayed with me for a while but when I knew I couldn't get out by myself, I asked her to find you and Nick. I knew she'd do it,' he said confidently.

Nick looked down proudly at Moss. 'Two real live rescues in one night! You're awesome, Moss. Now who says you're not up to Grade Five?' He turned to his mum. 'Just wait until Uncle John hears about this!'

Back at the centre, Miss Fraser bandaged James's ankle and gave him some tablets to help ease the swelling. 'You'll have to rest it for a few days,' she said. 'Which means no more trekking for you this holiday.'

James groaned with disappointment but soon cheered up when Mandy and Nick told him that the SSPCA were coming to Heathwylde the next day.

'I'm sure they'll close Mr Mackay down,' Mandy said while she towelled her hair dry. 'It looks like the worst is over for the ponies.'

At that moment, Mrs Russell came in with a tray of hot chocolate and biscuits. 'There's justice in the world after all,' she smiled, handing James a mug. 'And I guess without you three, things wouldn't have worked out this way.' She looked at Nick. 'Not that I'm condoning horse theft, mind you,' she quickly reminded him. 'Next time you want to stage a dramatic rescue, tell me or the police first, won't you?'

Nick grinned at his mother. 'Or I can send my rescue dog out to do it for me,' he joked, running his fingers through Moss's shaggy coat.

Miss Fraser stood up and reached for her jacket that had been drying on a rack in front of a fan heater. 'I'd better go over to Heathwylde again,' she said. 'The grooms have really got their hands full, and I'd feel much happier if I could show them what to do.' She glanced at the clock on the mantelpiece. 'Goodness! Look at the time. They must think I've abandoned them.'

It was close to midnight but Mandy didn't feel at all tired – even after everything they'd been through that night. And there was still more to be done. Heathwylde was full of ponies needing urgent attention. 'Wouldn't you like some extra help?' she asked Miss Fraser.

The vet was pulling on her jacket. She stopped and looked at Mandy. 'You must be worn out after crossing the mountain twice tonight.'

Mandy shook her head. 'I'm fine, really,' she insisted.

'Me, too,' Nick added quickly. 'I've got tonnes of energy left. And two extra pairs of hands should make a big difference.'

Miss Fraser glanced at Mrs Russell. 'Nick's right. There's a lot he and Mandy could do, especially as they're obviously much better with horses than Mr Mackay's staff. Would you mind if they came along? I'll bring them home when we're finished.'

Nick's mum hesitated.

'Please, Mum,' Nick implored. 'It's not as if we have to get up for school in the morning.'

'Or for a trek,' Mandy put in, shooting James a

sympathetic smile. Although Mandy would have loved to go out for another ride the next day, she wouldn't have dreamed of leaving James on his own.

Mrs Russell began gathering up the mugs. 'If you're both prepared to feel like zombies tomorrow,' she said with a grin, 'then far be it from me to keep you here!'

They piled into Miss Fraser's Land-rover and bumped along the mountain road to the stud farm. When they eventually pulled up in front of the house, Mandy noticed a curtain being drawn aside in an upstairs room. A face appeared in the window – Mr Mackay's. Mandy could almost feel his eyes boring into them as he watched them going over to the paddocks. She turned to Nick. 'He must be really furious to see us back here.'

'That's just too bad,' said Nick. 'He's had this coming to him for a long time.'

By contrast, the grooms were very relieved to see them again. The wind had died down a little but it was still raining steadily, which hampered the men in their efforts. They had rounded up the six pregnant mares and brought them into the stable yard but still had to clean out some stalls for them.

'Some of these are due to foal very soon,' said Miss Fraser, examining the ponies. 'We need to get them stabled quickly and give them a good feed.'

'We can clean out the stables,' Mandy volunteered. 'And feed the ponies.'

'Thanks,' said one of the grooms. 'We'll see to the other horses in the paddocks.'

Working quickly, Mandy and Nick swept out a row of six stalls. They found some clean straw in the yard and spread it on to the floors of the stables. Then they led the mares inside.

'They look really relieved,' Mandy sighed when the ponies were finally settled in. She went to the end of the row where a dun mare was looking out at her over the top of the stable door. She patted the pony's neck. 'Now you can look forward to having your foal,' she said softly to her.

With the mares taken care of, Mandy and Nick helped to carry fresh water out to all the paddocks. Finally, when they'd done all they could for the ponies that night, it was time to go home.

But Nick had one last task. 'Hold on,' he said,

heading back towards the stables. 'I want to check on Gandalf again. Coming, Mandy?' he called to her.

'You bet!' said Mandy.

The young stallion appeared to be fast asleep when they came to his stall. But he sensed their presence and slowly opened his big brown eyes.

'Feeling better now, Gandalf?' asked Nick, running his hand down the pony's neck.

Gandalf responded with a contented snort. Then he stretched his neck over the stable door and nuzzled Mandy's hair.

'And tomorrow, the SSPCA are coming to sort everything out,' said Mandy as Gandalf breathed warm puffs of air down her neck. 'You'll be in safe hands at last.'

Ten

Mandy stretched and opened her eyes. Daylight filled the room. She reached over to the bedside table for her watch. 'Half past nine!' she gasped. She threw off the duvet, realising only too late that MacDonald was curled up on the bed next to her.

'Sorry, Mac,' she said, quickly smoothing the big tabby cat who glared at her indignantly. 'But it's time we got up, you know – even if you don't have much to do today!'

Mandy washed and dressed hastily, all the time thinking back to the night before. What an amazing series of events! And to think that it had all turned out so well. Except for poor James, she thought as she hurried downstairs.

The others were all in the dining room tucking into a late breakfast. Mandy was very hungry. It seemed ages since she'd last eaten. She sat down next to James, who looked pointedly at his watch, then grinned at her.

'Anyone would think you'd had a late night or something,' he said.

'Makes a change for you to be awake before me,' Mandy joked back. Then, more seriously, she asked, 'How's your ankle?'

'Not too bad,' James said, pulling his bandaged foot out from under the table. 'I expect I'll live!'

After breakfast, Mrs Russell drove the three of them as well as Moss and Fern over to Heathwylde.

'How did the jeep get back to Kincraig?' Mandy asked, remembering that they'd left it at the stud farm last night.

'The grooms brought it over first thing this morning,' Mrs Russell told her, driving through the gates to the farm.

Mandy couldn't wait to see all the ponies again.

'We're just in time!' she exclaimed. It looked like the SSPCA had already been there for a while.

Two enormous horseboxes were parked in the stable yard and uniformed SSPCA inspectors were leading some ponies out of the paddocks. The two grooms from the night before were helping, looking tired and subdued.

'Obviously they've seen enough to make them decide to remove the horses,' Mrs Russell said, parking the jeep nearby.

'Where are they going to take them?' Mandy asked.

'Back to the society's own yard, I expect,' Mrs Russell replied. 'They'll stay there until new homes are found for them.' She looked round the yard. 'There's Jane's Land-rover. I expect she's checking the pregnant mares to make sure they're fit to travel. I'll go and help her.' With Fern trotting next to her, she went over to the stable block.

'Let's help to load the ponies,' suggested Nick. 'Then we'll go and see Gandalf.'

Mandy and Nick hurried over to the horseboxes. Halfway there, Mandy realised she'd forgotten about James. She stopped and turned. He was hobbling along some distance behind them. Moss was walking slowly at his side, her eyes glued to him. It was almost as if she was afraid he'd come to more harm.

'Sorry,' Mandy called, waiting for James to catch up with them.

'That's OK,' smiled James. 'My guardian angel's with me anyway.'

Mandy and Nick helped to lead the first group of ponies up the ramp while James stood by, talking soothingly to those waiting their turn.

Then it was time to fetch the pregnant mares from the stables. 'We'll bring them over for you,' Mandy offered.

The SSPCA team were only too pleased to have some help. There were still several other ponies for them to bring across from the paddocks.

In the stable block, Nick's mum and Miss Fraser were busy with a mare in the third stall. Mandy watched with the others for a minute while Miss Fraser examined the pony, then she decided to go and see the dun mare at the end of the row.

Unlike the night before, the pony wasn't peering out over the top of the door. *She's probably having a good feed*, Mandy guessed, thinking with pleasure how happy the mares must have been to find themselves safely indoors at last.

She stood on her toes and looked in over the door. The mare was lying down at the back of the stable. For a second, Mandy thought she was asleep but then she saw a little black heap lying in the straw behind her. Mandy caught her breath. 'You've had your foal!' she whispered excitedly.

Not wanting to disturb them, Mandy stepped back quietly then joined the others and told them the news. 'I think she must only just have given birth,' she said. 'They're both still on the ground.'

'I'll go and see if they're all right,' said Miss Fraser, picking up her bag and hurrying away.

Mandy and the others waited anxiously for the vet to come back. But when she did, she was smiling. 'Mandy's right,' Miss Fraser said. 'The foal's barely ten minutes old. And he looks just fine! He's very handsome – black with a tiny white star on his forehead.'

Mandy was longing to have a close look at the little foal but she knew that he and his mother needed to be on their own for a while. She also realised that they'd have to be very carefully handled when they were moved.

Miss Fraser echoed her thoughts. 'We'll load

them last,' she said. 'I want the foal standing strongly and suckling before we even think about taking them out of here.'

The news of the foaling seemed to lift everyone's spirits. 'It's a new beginning for all of these horses,' said one of the SSPCA inspectors as they loaded the rest of the mares into one of the horseboxes. He made five ticks on a list attached to his clipboard.

'You'll have to add another pony to that list,' James said to him.

The man smiled. 'Indeed!' he said, making a note about the foal. Then he ran his eyes down the list. 'Right then, Gandalf's Secret is next.'

Nick must have been preparing himself for this moment. 'I'll get him,' he said, and Mandy noticed a catch in his voice. It was going to be hard for Nick to say goodbye to Gandalf after everything the two of them had been through together.

Nick picked up a lead rope and went to the stable. He returned minutes later with Gandalf. The pony was still lame, but he looked alert and well rested.

'I'll just check his foot one more time,' decided Miss Fraser.

'Let me take the dressing off,' Nick said quickly. While one of the inspectors held Gandalf, he carefully lifted the stallion's hoof, then stripped off the thick bandage.

Miss Fraser examined the injury. 'There's certainly no sign of an infection so I don't think I'll bother with another poultice. I'll just leave nature to take its course now.'

Gandalf seemed relieved to be free of the bulky dressing and whickered contentedly when Nick gently lowered his hoof to the ground.

The inspectors led the stallion over to the horsebox. 'Your turn now, boy,' he said, patting Gandalf gently to urge him up the ramp. 'It'll be a bit crowded where you're going, but it won't be forever. We'll soon find you a new home.'

Nick turned away, looking upset at the thought of seeing Gandalf leave.

Mandy tried to console him. 'Perhaps you'll be able to find out where he goes eventually so that you can visit him sometimes,' she said.

'I'd rather not visit him,' Nick said quietly.

Mrs Russell overheard him. 'You mean you'd prefer to have access to him all the time,' she said kindly. 'At Kincraig.'

Nick nodded.

'Funnily enough, I've just been having the same thoughts myself,' said Mrs Russell cheerfully. She turned quickly to the SSPCA team. 'It struck me when you mentioned that your yard is going to be rather crowded that we could help you out there. We have plenty of room at our trekking centre for another pony. Perhaps you'd let us give Gandalf a temporary home?' She ran her hand along Gandalf's back. 'I can assure you that our ponies are well cared for.'

'And I can vouch for that,' put in Jane Fraser.

The inspectors looked at one another and nodded. 'Actually, that's not a bad idea,' said one man. 'We're going to be pretty stretched looking after all of these horses as it is.'

'So, if that's all right, I'll fill in any necessary paperwork,' said Mrs Russell, 'then go back for my horsebox.' She turned to Nick and with a glint in her eye said, 'And who knows, we might even be allowed to give Gandalf a permanent home.'

Nick was jubilant. 'Thanks, Mum!' he said, hugging her tightly. Then he ran to Gandalf who was still standing at the bottom of the ramp and threw his arms around his neck. 'You're coming home with us,' he said, 'and this time, I don't have to steal you!'

Mandy gave Nick a triumphant thumbs-up and he replied with a grin that was so broad it seemed to split his face in half.

After filling in some forms, Mrs Russell drove away leaving Mandy, James and Nick to wait with Gandalf. Miss Fraser supervised the loading of the mare and her foal, then joined the three friends and Moss.

The SSPCA team closed the doors of the two big horseboxes, then turned and waved before climbing into the cabs. With a roar of powerful engines, the heavily laden vehicles pulled off.

As the dust began to settle in the driveway, Mandy thought about Mr Mackay. There had been no sign of him yet that morning. She glanced up at the window where she'd last seen him looking out. Just like the night before, he was staring sullenly down at them. He shook his head dejectedly, then turned away from the window and disappeared.

Nick had spotted him too. He leaned across and patted Gandalf who was blissfully cropping the green lawn. 'Let's hope you won't have to see him ever again, boy,' he said with a satisfied grin.

'We couldn't have hoped for things to turn out better,' said James, sitting down on a straw bale to rest his ankle.

'But it might have turned out very differently if Moss hadn't found Gandalf in the ditch,' Mandy pointed out.

'Yeah. And imagine if she hadn't come to my rescue too when *I* got stuck,' grinned James.

Miss Fraser was stroking Moss's head. 'She was quite the hero,' she agreed. 'In fact, two real life rescues in one night is very impressive for such a young dog.'

'I just wish the judges who assessed her could hear about it,' said Nick. 'Then they'd know what she's really made of.'

Miss Fraser turned to Nick and said thoughtfully, 'I think that can be arranged.'

Nick stared at her. 'What do you mean?'

'Simply that I'll tell everyone on the committee of the Rescue Dog Association just how good she is. You see, I'm part of the assessment team, and I don't think Moss should have to wait six months before she can try for Grade Five again,' Miss Fraser explained.

Mandy couldn't have agreed more. As far as she was concerned, Moss had more than proved herself.

Miss Fraser continued. 'In fact,' she added, 'the organisation desperately needs dogs like her. It would be a terrible waste if Moss couldn't be called out right away in an emergency.'

Nick looked stunned. 'So what do you think the committee will do?' he asked.

'I'm going to recommend that Moss has another chance to qualify next week,' answered Miss Fraser. 'And that she has to go on only two runs instead of four, seeing as she's already completed two very convincing ones!'

Mandy felt as if she would burst with happiness. Things just kept getting better!

For the trip back to Kincraig, Mandy and Nick squeezed into the trailer with Gandalf. The stallion stood calmly throughout the journey, pulling contentedly at a well-filled haynet.

'What a difference to the last time we saw him in a horsebox,' Mandy remarked to James when they arrived at the trekking centre and led the stallion out into the open.

The Kincraig ponies must have picked up the scent of the newcomer for they galloped over to the fence and peered inquisitively at the little procession that was heading towards the yard. The ponies whinnied and snorted when they saw Gandalf and he, in turn, pricked up his ears and stared with interest at them.

'It would be nice if we could introduce them all now,' said Nick. 'But I guess it won't hurt Gandalf to be on his own a little longer.'

'Mmm,' agreed Mrs Russell. 'Letting a stallion loose with a bunch of mares and geldings wouldn't be a particularly good idea!'

They took Gandalf into the stable yard where Morag was waiting. She'd prepared a stable already. 'I thought he'd appreciate this one,' she said, as Nick led Gandalf inside. 'It's roomy and has a fine view of the mountains.'

'And it's a bit nicer than the stable where I had to hide him,' said Nick, unclipping the lead rope.

Gandalf looked around his new surroundings. Then with a snort, he grabbed up a mouthful of hay from the rack and started chewing happily.

'Well, it doesn't look like he's going to be pining for his old home,' smiled Mrs Russell. 'So I think

we can leave him to settle in while we go and have a late lunch.' She caught Nick's eye. 'I haven't forgotten Moss. She deserves a treat too. I've got two enormous bones for her and Fern.'

But, even though they were all ravenous, lunch had to be delayed. Just as they reached the house, a car drove up and a man and a woman climbed out. They were carrying cameras and notebooks.

'We're from the *Aberford Herald*,' said the young man with a friendly smile. 'One of our contacts at the SSPCA told us about the goings-on at Heathwylde and we'd like to interview you all.'

The other reporter bent down and patted Moss. 'He also said something about a search and rescue dog staging two rescues in one night. Is this the heroic animal?'

Nick smiled proudly. 'Yes. Moss was fantastic!'

The reporters followed them inside and asked dozens of questions before taking photographs of everyone. Mandy supported James while he stood bravely on his wonky ankle, then helped him tell the story of their dramatic midnight adventures.

'Well, that should do it,' said the woman, taking one last shot of Nick and Moss. 'This will probably make the front page tomorrow.'

The telephone began to ring and Mrs Russell went to answer it. She came back a few minutes later. 'We're going to make the news on TV, too,' she announced, looking rather stunned. 'That was a reporter from the local TV station. He's also heard what's been going on and wants to come and interview us tomorrow. It looks like we're in for some wonderful publicity.'

'That's brilliant!' Mandy exclaimed. 'You're going to be famous!' She could hardly believe how well everything was turning out; not just for Gandalf and Nick, but for Moss and the trekking centre too.

After taking a few photographs of Gandalf, the reporters drove away. Then, just when Morag was at last bringing out the lunch, the telephone rang again.

'I'll get it,' said Nick. He returned a few moments later. 'What did you say about publicity, Mum?' he grinned. 'Someone's ringing up about the advert you put in the paper the other day.'

'Oh good,' said Mrs Russell and she hurried into the office to take the call. She came back smiling happily. 'A family of five has just booked in for next week,' she said.

'I wonder what will happen when the paper comes out tomorrow?' said Nick. 'And after the TV people have interviewed us?'

'With any luck, we'll be inundated with enquiries,' said Mrs Russell.

There were no further interruptions so they were all able to enjoy their lunch at last. Then, after they'd cleared away the dishes and washed up, Nick winked at Mandy and James and knelt down next to the sleeping Moss. 'How about another run to see to Gandalf, girl?' he whispered.

In a blink of an eye, Moss was on her feet. She stared attentively at Nick, waiting for him to give her the directions she needed.

'It's all right,' Nick said, patting her affectionately. 'No long trek for you today. We only have to go as far as the stables now.'

'That's right,' Mandy agreed. 'Gandalf's safe in his new stable. And hopefully he'll never need to be rescued again.'